THE LAST WIFE

MATT MCGREGOR

INKUBATOR
BOOKS

Published by Inkubator Books
www.inkubatorbooks.com

Copyright © 2025 by Matt McGregor

ISBN (eBook): 978-1-83756-561-0
ISBN (Paperback): 978-1-83756-562-7
ISBN (Hardback): 978-1-83756-563-4

PROLOGUE

I'm upside down, looking at her body on the cobblestones below.

I imagine that she has burst open, like a melon dropped from a high bench. But the truth is, I can't see much from up here.

She's probably dead. If she isn't, she will be by morning. No one's coming for her. Just like no one would be coming for me.

I feel my body lurch upwards a few inches, then slip back down. I let out an involuntary yell.

Jesus Christ. That was too close.

Next time that happens, I'll be joining her. Another melon burst open on the cobblestones.

I look away from the body to the historic town of Rosford. You can see the shops from here, the medical centre, the pharmacy, the bank. Everyone insists that Rosford is idyllic. *What a place to raise children*, they say.

Not me, though.

If it were up to me, I'd burn it all to the ground.

"Grab the ledge!" screams the woman holding my leg. "You're too heavy!"

I fumble for the ledge and try to take some of my weight. I don't have a strong grip, but when the woman pulls again, she gets enough momentum to send me tumbling over the fence.

I land on my back, then quickly scramble up to see who saved my life. I want to thank her. I should be dead.

But then I see who it is, and I freeze.

She has the gun — and she's pointing it at my head. Her hands are shaking wildly. If her finger slips just a little, I'll be dead.

I can't die. Not yet. Not until I'm finished.

"You killed her!" she screams.

I don't deny it. She saw it happen.

"Let me explain," I say, trying to keep my voice calm. How am I going to talk my way out of this? She saw everything. I'm a killer, and she knows it.

"I'm going to call the police." Her free hand fumbles in her pockets, the gun swinging wildly.

"No police!" I insist, but this doesn't stop her.

How can I explain the truth? I only have a few hours. If the police come, it will be too late. It will all be over.

It can't be. Not yet.

I've killed once.

And before this night is done, I need to kill again.

PART 1

CHAPTER ONE

"No. Way," I say, going through the french doors into the backyard. Though backyard isn't the right word — this isn't a square of grass for kids to play in. It's an enormous garden, manicured to perfection, with rows of peonies, lilies, and hydrangeas. "What a dream."

Lachlan sneezes. "If it were just me, we'd be living in an apartment in Manhattan. These flowers drive me crazy."

"But you put up with it." I take a beat. "For our blossoming romance."

"Blossoming divorce if you keep up these puns, Olivia Gibson," Lachlan mutters, before taking my hand. "Come on, you haven't seen the best bit."

Olivia Gibson. I'm still getting used to the new name. At the doctor's office the other day, Dr. Yang had to repeat my name four times before I looked up from my magazine.

"It's enormous," I say, as he leads me down a winding path, around a hedge, to a white wooden building. From the house I'd thought it was a garden shed — but as I get closer, I realize that it's a small chapel.

"What's this?" I ask, nervously. I wonder if this is when I find out my husband is actually a religious zealot. We'd never talked about religion, though our shotgun wedding — which not even my own mother attended — didn't exactly scream 'I have my own personal chapel and pray six times a day.'

But as my mother would have said — if she had the chance — we barely knew each other.

"This is where we pray," he says solemnly.

"Um, darling—"

"Twice daily. To your new god."

"There's a new god?" I mutter. "I really need to read a newspaper."

"This is actually the home of my new religion. Lachlanastrianism."

"Lachanastrianism? Rolls off the tongue, doesn't it?"

"It's sweeping the nation."

"Let me guess. We worship — you?"

"Who else?" He takes my hand and looks solemnly into my eyes. "Will you be the mother of my church? It's a big responsibility."

"What do I get out of it?"

"You get to sleep with the father of the church."

"Well, cult leaders are actually kind of hot," I say. "But you'd better watch your back. One day, I might assassinate you. Strangle you with rosary beads. Take power for myself."

"You're a worry sometimes, Mrs. Gibson." Next to the door, a bee whines in the grass. Before I can protest, Lachlan squashes it with his custom leather shoe. He notices my look and shrugs. "It's a mercy kill. Come on in."

He pushes open the door and I step into a large room filled with sunlight. There are a half-dozen pews, and at the far end, an altar and pulpit. Behind them, a stained glass window about six feet high depicts a bearded man kneeling next to a young woman, eyes downcast.

"Jesus," I whisper.

"Exactly."

"What is this place?"

"The original owner was a particularly religious man and wanted somewhere to pray. He bought this from a small town and installed it in his garden. So now we have our own chapel."

"That's wild."

"I know. But come, look."

He takes my elbow, and we walk past the pews to the front corner, where an easel stands in front of an enormous window. Beside the easel, there's an array of paints and brushes laid out neatly on a wooden table.

"No. You didn't!" I turn to him, my stomach weak with excitement. "This is so thoughtful."

"I don't really know much about art, but I asked someone at the shop, and they said this was the best."

I kiss him on the cheek, then go to the window. At the end of the garden is a low fence, and beyond that is a meadow of wildflowers. In the distance, I can make out the light dancing off a small creek.

"Lachlan—" I feel light, as if I were a newborn deer, with no memories, no responsibilities, no knowledge of the world.

"Isn't it something?" he asks, stepping behind me. "Imagine our kids playing here. Wouldn't it be perfect?"

Kids. I feel lightheaded. "That's the word."

"Mew!" We both turn to see Homer trotting alongside the pews, his orange coat shining in the sunlight. When I pat him, his fur is hot to the touch.

"Do you like it here?" I mutter, scratching him under the chin.

"Mew!"

"Better than our apartment in Queens? Surely not." I turn to Lachlan. "I think you have another happy customer."

His face is impassive. He hasn't been a fan of Homer since the cat took a nap on his freshly dry-cleaned suits. Twice.

"He'll need a bell."

"No!" I protest. "That's cruel."

"There are protected birds in the meadow and this guy's a killer."

"This guy?" Homer leaps down and struts towards the front of the church. He stretches his paws against the altar, then leaps onto it. "I think he heard you. Look, he's insulted."

"I mean it."

"So do I. Let me look into it, OK? I'll find something that doesn't turn him into a total eunuch."

"Isn't he already a eunuch?"

"That's my point. First we take his balls, then we stop him hunting? Might as well stuff him and put him on the mantelpiece."

While I watch Homer stretch out, I feel Lachlan's breath on my neck. He wraps his arm around my waist and kisses me below the ear. His light afternoon stubble tickles, but it feels nice. I close my eyes and let him continue — until the predictable happens.

When his hand moves up to my breast, I pull away.

"Mr. Gibson! We can't. Look who's watching us."

"Homer?"

"No, Him!" I point to the stained glass. "Our lord and

savior. I don't think He'd appreciate us copulating on the pews."

"I didn't know you believed in all that."

"Even if I don't, I believe in bad juju."

"Juju?" He touches my hip and kisses me softly. "Really?"

"Karma. Respect. I don't know. It just seems wrong."

"Don't worry," he whispers, before kissing me again. "It's not consecrated anymore."

I forget myself for a moment as he touches me. As usual, his hands move slowly across my body — I would say *expertly*, though I try not to think about how he earned that expertise. It's only when I feel him working the zip on my dress that I pull away.

"Not here," I say, pulling it back up over my shoulder. "It's not right. It's sacred or something. Let's just go inside."

"No. Here." He pulls at his shirt, then tugs the dress down hard so that it falls to the ground. "This is sacred," he whispers in my ear.

Twice more I say no, but he keeps undressing me. When we're naked, he reaches under the nearest pew and pulls out a mattress.

"You planned this," I say, lying down.

"I'm just prepared."

"You're always prepared. Like a good Boy Scout."

"That's why you love me," he says, rolling on a condom. "And is a Boy Scout really the image you want in your head right now?"

"Come on then. Naughty little boy."

I'm almost ashamed at how little time it takes for me to finish. I tell myself that it isn't the setting — I'd rather not have 'screwing in chapels' as my fetish — so much as this day, the first in our new home. It's perfect.

Too perfect, as it turns out. Because as he buries his face into my neck and races to catch up, I look up at the ceiling and see a name. It's been painted over, but in the afternoon light and from this angle, I can make it out, clear as day.

The name of another woman.

Yasmin.

CHAPTER TWO

SIX MONTHS EARLIER

"Table six! Olivia, come on."

"I have table four," I say.

"Six! Now!"

Marco is standing with two sizzling fajitas. I drop the appetizers and take the two main courses to the waiter, Alistair. Normally he's waiting in the wings of the restaurant, but I see that he's busy with another table.

Marco says we have sixty seconds to get from the kitchen to the table, and I've used up most of that already. I look at the customers — a tall man in a suit with a young blonde woman. I already know the type. He's rich, she's hot, and they're both dull as ditchwater.

But at least they can afford to eat here, a voice says. *While you had to beg to even work here.*

Fair enough. I'm not even a waitress. I'm just a food runner. My entire job is to clean tables and take food from the kitchen to the real waiters, so they can stay in the main restaurant and respond instantly to their customers.

With the size of the tips in a place like this, it's the only kind of service work that can pay my share of the rent. Some-how, this has become my grand ambition — to graduate from food runner to waitress. I'd done it before, but was fired from my last gig after the head waiter got handsy on the floor and I slapped him in front of everyone.

It was the first time I'd ever hit anyone. I didn't even know I was capable of it till then.

Marco knew my experience, but he also knew I was desperate, and he had decided to make me earn it. So, I'm not allowed to serve anyone yet. I have to prove myself, living on whatever fraction of tips my waiter Alistair decides to grace me with at the end of each shift.

But here I am, with the clock ticking on the fajitas. So I decide to go for it.

"Here you are," I say.

The man immediately looks up at me. "You look different."

"The chef said I should get these to your table as soon as possible."

"Amazing." He keeps staring. "Listen, resolve an argu-ment for us. Amanda here says that she's living her dream. She's a model on social media. I don't actually know how that works, but I don't think that's any sort of dream. Do you?"

I can see Alistair is finished with his table and is watching me from the wings. The longer this goes on, the worse my tips are going to be. But I also know the golden rule: When the customer wants to talk, you talk.

"I think people can choose their own dreams."

"I think people lie to themselves. I think they have real dreams as children, and then forget them somehow. What's your dream?"

"You don't think this is my dream?"

He laughs, then catches himself. "Serving rich assholes like me?"

I glance at the blonde woman, who looks increasingly annoyed by this interaction. "Give Alistair a nod if you need anything else."

I turn to leave when he grabs my arm. "You didn't tell me your dream. What do you want to be when you grow up?" I look at his hand until he takes it away. "Sorry. But it's a sincere question."

Before I can stop myself, I say, "A rich asshole like you." The woman snorts, while the man gives a booming laugh, loud enough to get the attention of half the restaurant.

Half the restaurant — and Alistair. I can see him glaring at me. I try to extract myself from the table, when he says, "You want to be an artist."

"How do you know?"

"This is not a pipe." He points to the cursive writing tattooed just above my elbow. "That's cool."

"No it isn't." Damian still made fun of me for it. He called it 'basic', which essentially meant that someone normal might actually recognize it. "I got it done at art school. I don't even like Magritte."

"*The Treachery of Images*," he says. "The man had a talent for titles. Who's your favorite artist, then?"

I glance at Alistair, who is glaring at me like I'm screwing his boyfriend right in the middle of the restaurant. I feel like I can see the vein throbbing in his neck from 30 feet away. I already know what's going to happen. He's going to report me to Marco, and it will then be a coin flip as to whether I'm fired or not.

"Frida Kahlo."

"Interesting choice."

"Yeah, fascinating," his date interjects.

I smile at her, then use the interruption to leave the table before I cause the vein in Alistair's neck to burst open like a tube of paint.

THAT COIN FLIP? It doesn't go my way. At the end of the shift, Marco yells at me in front of the rest of the staff. It's not the first time I've been yelled at in front of other people as an adult, though it's still an uncanny feeling, like I've been teleported back to high school. He says I risked the reputation of the restaurant by doing a job I wasn't qualified to do. I think I might have a chance of surviving, but then he declares to everyone that I was visibly flirting with one of the customers.

"This is inexcusable!" he declares, glaring at the assembled group like he's a general on the front lines.

I know better than to argue back. The decision has already been made, and there's no point pretending I have any power in this situation. Still, when he fires me, I feel like I've been hit by a truck, because I know what it means. Another round of applications and interviews. More time spent at the bottom of the ladder, working my way up.

My face feels hot, but I wait until I'm on the street to start crying. I'd never give Marco the satisfaction. I also can't pretend this isn't a disaster. I'm pushing thirty, and the only practical skill I've tried to develop — serving other people — is one that I'm constantly finding out I suck at.

I'm starting to walk to the subway when I hear a voice.

"Are you OK?"

I look up to see a man leaning against a large black car.

It's nearly midnight and I know I should walk the other way, but something about him seems familiar.

"I'm fine."

"Can I give you a ride?"

"Excuse me?"

He laughs — and then I recognize him. The man that got me fired.

"It's OK. I can get the train."

"At this hour?"

"I do it every night. It's fine."

"Please. I insist. If it makes you feel better, I'll just get you a taxi." He hands over his phone. "Just put in your address."

I stare at the phone. There's no way in hell I'm giving this guy my address. But I'm also too exhausted to figure out how to delicately extract myself from the situation.

So I decide not to be delicate.

"What are you doing here? You left with the blonde girl an hour ago."

"I dropped her home. Then I came back."

Run, I tell myself. *This guy's going to chop you into pieces. He's a psycho.*

"Why?" I ask. My voice is shaking. I know I'm not in any immediate danger — this is Manhattan and the streets are hardly empty — but I also have no experience with rich guys.

"To talk to you."

"I'm not interested," I say, and begin to walk off.

"Please." His footsteps are heavy behind me. "I know what you're thinking. But there was something back there in the restaurant. I felt it. A connection."

"I don't have connections with people who are on dates," I snap. "And that so-called connection just got me fired."

He jogs to catch up. Soon he's standing in front of me. He's tall and remarkably handsome, with broad shoulders and short blond hair, parted to the side. But at the moment, all I can see is a large man who's not letting me pass.

I put on my best I'm-about-to-kick-you-in-the-balls voice. "Please move out of the way!"

"Have a drink with me," he says, quickly. "I'm sorry, I'm being weird. It's just — the women I see these days, they — they're not like you."

"They're hot?"

He smiles. "You're hot, too. But that's just it. You're quick."

"This city is full of smart women."

"My name's Lachlan," he says, quickly.

"I didn't ask," I snap. "And there's brilliant, beautiful, single women everywhere you look. If you can't find one, then you can't be looking very hard."

"One drink."

"I said no. Now move."

"I give in. But I still feel bad. Let me make it up to you and get you a taxi." He hands me his phone again. I suddenly feel too exhausted to care if he's a serial killer. I have no job, no money, no life. And my feet are aching. "I'm sorry you lost your job."

"It wasn't your fault," I mutter. I take the phone and as I type in my address in Queens, the sleeve of my dress edges up. When I hand the phone back, I see him frowning.

"Who did this to you?"

I pull my sleeve back down. I had covered the bruise in concealer multiple times during the night, but it had clearly rubbed off.

"I just banged my arm. You know what working in restaurants is like." I pause for a second. "Maybe you don't."

"I didn't always work in finance," he says. "I bussed tables through college."

"Just like a real working man."

"That's right. Never got a bruise like that, though. How'd you bump into something and bruise the inside of your arm?"

I look down at his shoes, and can somehow tell that they've been custom made for his feet. Everything he's wearing seems to fit perfectly.

"What happened to your date?" I ask. "For real?"

"It didn't work out."

I can hardly believe my audacity, but I keep going. "Why not?"

"Someone took my breath away." I look over my shoulder, as if to check if she were standing behind me, and he laughs. "It's tragic, though."

"Why?"

"I think she probably has a boyfriend."

I'm wildly out of my depth. I've been hit on before, but it's nearly always crude and sleazy, especially when I'm working at a restaurant. Guys don't want to be romantic with a waitress — they want a quick rendezvous in the bathroom. But this guy is different. He's an adult. An actual, real-life man. He wears an analogue watch, black shoes, and a clean shirt. He shaves and looks like he cut his hair sometime in the last week. I bet he hasn't played video games since he was a kid. I bet he doesn't watch superhero movies or cartoons.

I feel like David Attenborough, stumbling onto a rare

antipodean parrot that scientists had universally agreed was extinct.

"You're right," I say, trying to keep the regret out of my voice. "She does."

He holds my gaze for a moment, and I think for a second that he's about to kiss me. But then he holds out his hand and a black car pulls up. This isn't a normal ride-share — it's a black Mercedes. He opens the door for me and double-checks that the driver has the right address.

I thought that was the last time I'd ever see him again.

CHAPTER THREE

The next morning, I'm sitting at our small table sketching. I know that I should be applying for jobs, but I'm desperate to hold onto this small routine. I haven't painted in over a year, but I'm scared that if I lose the ritual of drawing every morning then I might lose the ability to do it at all.

"You haven't progressed." I jump to find my boyfriend Damian standing in the doorway. "You're still stuck in that representational framework."

According to Damian, I'm insufficiently intellectual to be an artist. He likes to point this out to me every time he drinks, which is basically every day. Damian is an arts graduate from NYU, and most of his friends are — like him — musicians and artists living off their trust funds. For a time, I found this dedication to the arts wildly attractive. But lately, I've been wondering if that masks a more basic truth. Maybe Damian is just a pretentious asshole who drinks too much.

"You're just getting home," I say. I knew this would bait him but I couldn't help it. As he moves towards me, I smell the cloud of whiskey that nearly always surrounds him in the morning.

"Where were you? Waiting on the rich and powerful?"

Even though Damian's life is funded by his father, a wealthy property developer, he still claims to hate the rich.

"We don't all have a trust fund."

I immediately tense as I see his fists clench. I knew this would happen — so why did I taunt him? I guess because I knew it would happen anyway, no matter what I said or did. It was becoming routine, these little showdowns in the morning.

"You worthless piece of—" He strides across the room towards me. "I'm out there every night, playing every room in the state. I have courage. I'm actually brave. You're too scared to show your work to your own mother."

Before I can respond, he pulls me up from my chair and sends me stumbling across the room.

"Look at this trash," he says, picking up my sketch. "You don't have it, Olivia! Give it up! Get a real job."

"Give it back!" I launch at him to snatch the paper from his hands, but he dodges away. "I spent all morning on that."

He dances away from me towards the kitchen. While I scream at him, he opens the window and throws my drawing outside. I watch it float away, down to the noisy street below. As soon as the sketch is gone, I suddenly see my life — and Damian's — for exactly what it is, and it's ridiculous.

I start laughing. "You're pathetic."

I know what I'm doing. Damian can't stand to be laughed at. He storms towards me, and a second later I'm flying into the bookshelf. I slam into it with my shoulder and slide down to the floor, causing his copies of *Infinite Jest* and *Ulysses* to fall onto my head.

Great, I think. *There's another bruise I'll have to cover up.*

I wonder if this is the time he'll take it too far — whether he'll hurt me so badly I'll finally have to pack up and leave — when there's a knock at the door.

"If it's that bitch from downstairs—" he mutters. He turns to me. "Keep your mouth shut, OK?"

He walks across the room casually and opens the door. I'm surprised he isn't whistling. As usual, his mood has improved after beating me up. It's like he's just come back from therapy.

"Yes?" he says.

I take the chance to sit up and examine myself for broken bones. I pray that he hasn't done any serious damage. I don't have health insurance anymore, and can't afford a trip to the emergency room.

"Is Olivia here?"

I recognize his voice before I see him. It's the dude — no, the *man* — from last night. Lachlan.

"Who are you?"

"I'm looking for—" I stand up and hobble towards the door so I can confirm that it's him. "—Olivia. Is everything alright?"

"Hey, man," Damian says, trying to block Lachlan's view.

"I'm fine," I say. Though I'm strangely glad to see him, I can already tell that Damian is going to punish me for this after he leaves.

"You're bleeding." I dab my shirt with my hand. He's right — it's damp with blood. The corner of the shelf has sliced me along my shoulder. Before I can say anything, Lachlan steps into the apartment. "What happened?"

"Bro," Damian says, stepping into his way. A second later, Damian's sprawling across the floor, clutching his cheek. "What the hell?" he screams.

Lachlan ignores him like he's nothing more than a yapping terrier and kneels down beside me.

"Did he do this to you?" When I don't respond, he nods. "I knew it. Come with me."

"I can't," I whisper. "This is my home."

"It'll be OK."

"Bro, get out of my—" Damian begins, but a look from Lachlan shuts him up. Damian has the emaciated body of a drug addict. He's a lot stronger than me, but next to Lachlan he looks like a bag of bones.

"Come." He holds out his hand. "Let's get out of here."

I hesitate for a moment, calculating the odds. There's a small chance that he's a murderer. A big chance that he wants to sleep with me.

But he could also be a good guy. They exist, don't they?

Maybe it's time I take a chance and find out.

"Let me get my stuff." I pause. "My cat. I can't leave him."

"That's fine," he says. "Leave it. I'll have someone pick it up. I promise."

And so I take one last look at Damian, someone I still loved, and our tiny apartment, which had once seemed so romantic, so full of promise, and I leave.

A BLACK LUXURY CAR, just like the one he ordered me last night, is idling outside.

"Why did you come back?" I ask, as he opens the door for me.

"For you," he says, simply.

"I told you I had a boyfriend."

"And I told you we had a connection. I couldn't just ignore it."

"Bullcrap. You saw my bruise. You thought I needed rescuing."

"No," he says quickly. "I think you can take care of yourself."

"But I wasn't. I don't," I say, my voice barely above a whisper. We're leaving Queens and are soon entering the gridlock into Manhattan. As the car slows, I begin to panic. What have I done? I know that I needed to leave Damian, but couldn't I wait till I had an actual job, or a place to stay? He probably won't even give my half of the security deposit back.

"You can let me out wherever."

"Where are you going to sleep tonight?" I don't respond, and his voice becomes urgent. "You can't go back to him."

"It must be so simple for you." I turn to him, my eyes watering. "But we've been together for five years. We share a lease. And I love him, as weird and pathetic as that sounds. Plus, I don't have a job, or savings, or insurance. I'm going to be homeless. Do you get that? So I'm glad you got to be a hero, but real life isn't what it seems from your penthouse apartment. Sometimes we don't have choices."

"I don't believe that."

"I don't give a crap what you believe. It's my life. What the hell do you know? You're just a finance bro with a savior complex." I let out a cry of frustration. I've definitely made the wrong move. Damian's an asshole, but I need a roof over my head. I need to save some money. I need a goddamn *job*. "Who even are you? I must have lost my mind leaving with you."

We drive in silence towards the Upper East Side. I pick at my cuticles, wondering how I'm going to deal with Damian later tonight. I can already picture the accusations. His face close to mine, spittle flying from his mouth. His hands around my arms, shaking me. We eventually come to a stop at an apartment building one block over from Central Park.

"You're wrong," he says.

"What?"

"I don't live in a penthouse. And I'm not a bro, though I manage a few. I'm an adult, Olivia." He holds out his hand. "The world is much different than you think. Come with me. Let me show you."

I stare at him for a moment. Another coin flip. Either I go back to my boyfriend, who will definitely hurt me, but won't kill me; or I follow this man, who doesn't look like he'll hurt me, but is sounding more and more like a serial killer with every super-intense sentence that comes out of his mouth.

"You sound like someone from a romance novel. This isn't a *Fifty Shades of Grey* situation, is it?"

"I'm not a billionaire," he says.

"And I'm not a wide-eyed college student."

I stare at his hand until he starts laughing. "This is getting a little awkward. Just come inside, will you?"

"I'm not having sex with you," I announce louder than I intend.

He glances at the driver and snorts. "It's just a place to stay. Until you find a job and get back on your feet."

"No whips and chains? And you won't chop me into pieces and put me in the freezer?"

"I'll put all my dungeon gear away as soon as you come over. And there's no space in my freezer for a dismembered corpse, unfortunately."

"OK," I say, cracking a smile. "I'll come up."

CHAPTER FOUR

He's not lying. His apartment isn't the penthouse — it's three floors down, a colossal two-bedroom with high ceilings. Floor-to-ceiling windows stretch alongside the open-plan living room and kitchen, offering an unbelievable view of the surrounding buildings.

"No view of Central Park?" I ask.

"I told you I wasn't a billionaire."

"You're just a humble millionaire. Poor bub."

"Why do I suddenly regret asking you here?" He grins and I notice his teeth, which are perfectly straight and white. "I'm going to the little boy's. Help yourself to a drink."

After he leaves, I pour myself a water in the kitchen, then wander through to the living room. On the far wall is a floor-to-ceiling bookshelf. I take a closer look at the titles. Joyce. Woolf. Faulkner. The poetry of T.S. Eliot. Henry James. Shakespeare. Thucydides. Herodotus. Aeschylus. Sophocles.

And that's just the titles in English. There are books in French and German, too.

Not a single detective novel. No thrillers or sci-fi.

"Do you need a recommendation?"

I jump with shock, as if I've been caught hunting through his underwear drawer. "You've read all these?"

"They're just there to make me look smart. I'm just a dumb finance bro, you know?"

"Then how could you make a recommendation?"

He smiles again and moves close enough for me to smell his cologne. My knees go weak. I may be in a romance novel, after all. "You've got me. I've always been a bookworm."

"And a snob. Where's the Jack Reacher?"

"No." He gives a sniff. "That's not for me. I believe life is for intense experiences. I don't waste my time on light entertainment. I want to feel something. Don't you agree?"

I think of all the mindless pop music in my playlists, not to mention the endless array of romance novels and thrillers stocked into my e-reader. But despite all this, I nod — because I *want* to agree. I do want to live a more intense and meaningful life. I do want to be a serious, adult person who likes classical music and reads serious novels. After all, isn't that the kind of person who creates great works of art?

"I'm so glad. Because I have something to give you." He reaches into his jacket pocket and pulls out two tickets.

I squint at the writing. "The ballet?"

"Tonight. Will you accompany me?"

"Is this a date?"

"No, of course not. We're just friends."

"Are we now?" I pull off my jacket to reveal my blood-stained t-shirt. "I might stand out in this outfit, I'm afraid. And I don't have anything else to wear."

"Jesus, I'm sorry. I forgot all about that. Come." He holds out his hand. "Let me take a look at it."

I wave his hand away. "It's just a scratch. If you've got a Band-Aid, I can do it myself."

"Just a scratch? Nonsense." He digs around in the cupboards and comes back with a first aid kit and a bowl of water. "Let me do it. You'll be one-handed."

"Fine." I roll up the sleeve of my t-shirt. The wound is tiny — it really is just a scratch — but it's in an awkward position. "If you're trying to convince me you don't have a savior complex, this isn't helping."

"Shush." He dabs the wound with a ball of damp cotton wool, then applies a line of white cream. Up close, his hair is sprinkled with gray. I have a strange desire to run my hand through it. "Do you want a princess or a pussycat on your Band-Aid?"

"Shut up."

He puts on the Band-Aid — which I'm weirdly disappointed to see has neither a princess nor a pussycat on it — and then rolls down my sleeve. "Easy as that."

"Thanks," I say, immediately stepping away from him. I feel unsure of myself, as if every word and gesture carries a special weight and if I say the wrong thing, my life could change forever. "I mean it. You're being kind."

"You need to have higher expectations about how people treat you."

"That's true. But still. I'm not exactly surrounded by kind people."

"Well, they're idiots."

He stares at me with such intensity that I look down at my feet. What the hell is going on? Who talks like this?

"OK, Mr. Grey. That's enough." I go back to the living room and put my jacket on over my bloodstained top. "Still not quite ballet-worthy, I'm afraid."

"Ah!" He jogs down the hall. A minute later, he's carrying a dress wrapped in plastic. "I'm pretty sure this will be your size."

I stare at the dress, unsure of how to react. "Now I'm legit worried. Why does a single man have a dress in his closet?"

"It's my sister's. She stores it here so she can go out when she's in the city."

"Where does she live?"

"London."

I raise an eyebrow. "Finance?"

"The disease runs in the family, unfortunately."

I take the dress in my hands. It's gorgeous, a vintage Christian Dior that is probably worth more than my entire wardrobe twice over.

Scratch that. *Ten times* over.

"I should get a job in finance," I mutter. "This is unbelievable."

"No, it's entirely real," he says, then takes a small velvet box from his jacket pocket. "I thought you might want to wear these, too."

Inside are two diamond earrings. "She won't want me taking these."

"Don't worry. They were actually my mother's." When he sees my expression, he looks bashful. "I'm sorry, it's too much. I'm coming on too strong, aren't I?"

"Yes. But it's sweet, honestly. I'll wear them," I say. "Just don't get handsy during the ballet."

THAT EVENING, I'm standing in the lobby of The Met while Lachlan gets me a drink. I look up and feel a rush of astonishment to be standing here, in this place, with these people. Does everyone know that I don't belong here? Do they know I'm a fraud?

This isn't my New York City. My city is cramped apartments, trains to warehouse raves, tiny exhibitions catered by crackers and boxed wine. Whereas this New York was top-shelf liquor, Ivy League degrees, men with watches that could pay off my student loan.

"Here you go." He hands me a glass of something bubbly. "Cheers."

As we clink glasses, I look over my shoulder. "What the hell am I doing here? I think I've seen seventeen famous people since we got here."

"So what?"

"I don't belong."

"Please. You're the most beautiful woman here."

"Are you kidding?" I nod to my left. "That woman is a literal model."

"I'm not kidding."

He stares at me with so much intensity that I have to look away. I know it's just a line, but I can't help the rush of warmth I feel in my stomach. There's nothing wrong with this, is there? To let a man take you out and compliment you, even if you know that it isn't real? What's so bad about a lie if it makes me feel this way?

"This is so grown up," I mutter, as I follow him to our seats. They're on the floor, about fifteen rows back. I don't know much about seats at The Met, but these seem about as good as it gets.

And just as well, because the ballet is spectacular. I always thought I hated dance — but that's because all the dancers I saw were in tedious experimental shows in fifth-floor walk-ups. But this! The way their bodies moved across the stage, the elegance and athleticism and emotion! When it finishes, I feel like only a minute has gone by. I turn to Lachlan, who is watching me with a smile on his face.

"That was—" I trail off, lost for words.

"Yes, wasn't it?" He holds out his hand to help me up, and doesn't let go as he leads me through the crowd. When we get to the lobby, he moves his hand to the small of my back and whispers in my ear.

"You're the most beautiful woman I've ever seen."

I want to say that I'm immune to the cliches of seduction. I want to say I cringe and push his hand away. But the truth is, I make a decision then to fall for it, completely, without irony or resistance. I lean into him as we leave, and his hand wraps around my waist as we walk to his car.

He kisses me on the drive home, and when we get to his apartment, I let him undress me while I look out of his windows at the shining city.

Before I finish, he whispers in my ear, "You're perfect."

"WHAT ABOUT YOUR RULE?" he says, afterwards. We're lying in his impossibly comfortable bed under sheets with a ludicrously high thread count. I'm starting to realize that everything in Lachlan's life is the best it can be. The best apartment, the best seats, the best books and wine and clothes. "I thought you said no sex."

"I was playing hard to get." I turn on my side to face him. "You swept me off my feet. And I decided to let you."

"I'm glad you did."

"But that's all this is," I add, quickly. "You're very good at being romantic. But I just want to make sure that you know that I know that it's just a move." He frowns, so I keep talking. "I mean, you don't need to worry. I'm not really falling for all this. It's like being in a movie or something. But I know the real world is waiting for me."

"No moves."

"That feels like the biggest move of all."

"Why do I need to make a move now?" he asks, and I have to admit he has a point. I'm already naked. If he was the finance bro I thought he was, I'd be out on the street by now, waiting for the Uber he ordered five minutes after climaxing. "I meant everything I said. I feel a connection with you."

"Me too," I admit. "But honestly, I've just come out of a long relationship. I don't know if this is a good idea."

"You've just come out of an abusive relationship, you mean."

"Yeah, well. That doesn't change anything, does it? I don't know if I'm ready to jump into anything else."

"Ready? Why are you talking like a self-help podcast? This is your life, Olivia. You can't keep waiting to be ready. I'm here. Now."

"You're just a boy, lying naked next to a girl, asking her —" I trail off. I feel like I'm Wile E. Coyote sprinting off the edge of the cliff, my legs moving even though there's no ground beneath my feet. But unlike the cartoon, I know exactly how far I have to fall, and I'm not sure I'll be able to get up again.

I feel his hand on my cheek. "Don't run away from me," he says.

It's impossibly romantic and apparently sincere.

So I don't run.

I stay.

CHAPTER FIVE

My stuff arrives the next day, along with a frenzied-looking Homer. He spends the morning sniffing through the rooms and examining the deck, while I search online for jobs. By lunchtime, I've booked an interview for the next morning at an Italian place in Brooklyn. It's not fine dining, which means less money in tips, but it also means I can actually wait tables for real.

Lachlan comes home at six with two chicken salads. As I transfer them to plates on his dinner table, I see the receipt.

"You spent over a hundred dollars."

"Huh?"

"On salad?"

He snatches the receipt from my hand. "You're not supposed to look at that."

"You don't make friends with salad, Lachlan."

"What about girlfriends?" He opens an app on his phone, and soon classical music is playing in the background.

"What did you just say?"

"You heard me." He's looking at me again, with the same intensity as the night before, and I feel the same level of confusion. We've already had sex, so why the romance? He can't really have feelings for me — he doesn't even know me.

I go to the kitchen and take a Zoloft from my purse. "Slow down, OK?" I say, when I get back. "I'm barely more than twenty-four hours out of my last relationship."

"Not true." He wipes his face with a napkin. "That ended years ago. You were just too scared to leave."

"Christ, where do you get off telling me about my own life?"

He chews slowly, as if he's trying to pick his words carefully, though I know that's not true. Lachlan is the kind of guy who's never unsure of himself. "You deserve better."

"And that's you?"

"Yes." He smiles as if I've said something utterly moronic. "Clearly."

"This salad isn't worth fifty bucks." I toss my fork onto my plate. "And these designer chairs are uncomfortable."

"Any other complaints?" He's standing now and walking over to me. "What else is wrong?"

He touches my cheek. I look up at him, at his handsome face, and remember his body from last night — like a statue sculpted from marble — and I decide to give in, once again.

This isn't real, I tell myself. *But that doesn't make it wrong, does it?*

A rich, kind, handsome man. Who can blame me?

THE NEXT MORNING, it takes nearly an hour to get from the apartment to the restaurant in Brooklyn. I'm nervous, because I know that I won't be able to take much rejection. I've been in this situation before, and reckon I have a brief window — a week or two, maybe — before my confidence slides.

And I need money now. I'll need to save for a security deposit before I can move out of Lachlan's place. It's already getting weird. I've basically moved in with a stranger and within two days become completely dependent on him.

The restaurant is a generic Italian place, pizza and pasta, with framed prints of tourist attractions from across Sicily. On the far wall is a line of photos of old Italian-American stars, all in black and white. Frank Sinatra. Dean Martin. Joe DiMaggio.

A woman appears from the back, wiping her hands on her jeans. "Sorry, we open at twelve."

"Ah, no. I have an interview with—" I quickly check the name I've written on the inside of my arm. "Randolph?"

She frowns and goes back into the kitchen. A minute later, an older man with gray hair strides towards me.

"Olivia?"

"Yes, that's me."

"What are you doing here?" He sounds tired, frustrated.

"I called yesterday. We have an interview."

"What's wrong with you?"

I'm thrown by the aggression in his voice. "What do you mean?"

"You canceled. Your boyfriend canceled. Last night. Said you were violently ill."

"I don't have a boyfriend." My mind turns to Damian. Is he trying to sabotage my life? But that doesn't make any sense — there's no way he'd know about the interview. "There must have been a mistake."

"No mistakes," he says, shaking his head. "The position's filled."

"I came all the way out here," I protest. I wave the resume I had printed out at the library. "I have experience. Lots of it."

"One-strike policy for interviews." He shakes his head, and turns his back. "Good luck, lady."

I SPEND the rest of the day letting my anger stew.

Lachlan — he's the only one who knew about the interview. He must have canceled after I'd gone to sleep.

I rehearse the confrontation a thousand times in my head, my monologue becoming ever more righteous and triumphant. How dare he interfere with my life? In the last two days, he's made me lose my job, my boyfriend, and my apartment. And now he stops me even taking an interview?

As soon as he walks through the door, I'm striding towards him.

"You canceled my interview?"

"Hi." He hangs up his coat, before bending down to undo his laces.

"Answer me."

"It's been a long day, Olivia."

"Did you or did you not cancel my job interview?"

He kicks off his shoes and walks into the kitchen. "Yes, I canceled the interview."

"What the hell?" I realize that I'd been holding out hope that it might have been a misunderstanding. That he hadn't interfered with my life. "You have no right to do that!"

"You can do better, OK?" he says, with a sigh.

"What the hell do you know? I'm a waitress, Lachlan. It's literally my only professional experience."

"That's not true."

"What the hell do you know? Look at me! This is my life you're messing with. I've lost my job and my apartment, both because of you. And now you're stopping me from getting a new one."

"Are you done?"

"What did you say?"

There's a smile on his face, which only makes me even more enraged. I remind myself that this is someone who works on Wall Street. He probably puts thousands of people out of work every day before his morning coffee. He can't possibly understand how close ordinary people are to the edge. How fragile and precarious our lives are. I was one more bad day away from being literally homeless.

"I said, are you done?"

"The question is, are you done?" My voice is raised. "You need to stop."

"Helping you? No. Never. I care about you."

"You don't know me."

"I know how I feel. And I know you're capable of so much more. You're an artist, Olivia. Not a waitress. You shouldn't be wasting your time."

"What are you talking about? You saw a tattoo and you think I should be a professional artist? That's not a thing, Lachlan. Like five people have that job. On the planet. The rest of us just wait tables to pay off our debt from school."

"Go into the spare room."

"Stop—"

"Just go. Humor me."

I roll my eyes, but curiosity gets the better of me. I go through to the second bedroom, where a giant, oversized certificate is balanced against an easel.

"The Lachlan Gibson 2024 artist in residence is awarded to Olivia Yates," I read. "You've got to be kidding me. What is this?"

"Look, I know this is weird. But I have a feeling about you. And I know you're still figuring things out, but I think you should take a few months before you find another job. I've got you a studio down the street."

"My own studio."

"Correct."

"In *Manhattan*."

"That's right."

A week ago, I could barely pay my rent — and now this guy I know is offering me a studio in the most expensive real estate in America? It seems excessive. Frivolous. Honestly, I'd rather have the money. "This is too much."

"Please. Stay with me. Paint."

"It really is too much! I might not have any talent."

"I don't believe that. But now's your chance to figure it out. It's not forever. Just six months."

"I can't just live off you for six months. You don't understand. My mom would kill me. It'll set my gender back a hundred years."

He comes up and kisses me on the cheek. "Surely not that long? Maybe just a decade or two, tops."

"Lachlan."

"Just try it. Then I'll let you find a job."

"Let me?" I fold my arms. "You don't—"

"Poor choice of words!" He puts his hands together, as if

in prayer. "Pretty please? It'll make me feel better about selling my soul on Wall Street."

"Well," I say, picturing the studio. For the first time, I'd have my own space. It's too much to turn down. "I am concerned about your soul."

CHAPTER SIX

"Where are we going?"

"Just follow me."

We're in Central Park, holding hands. It's early summer and the sun is shining. It's just after five and Lachlan has taken off work early, something he hardly ever does. His firm recently laid off a thousand people — but Lachlan ended up with a promotion. Twice the work for a little more money, he says, though after a little digging I discover that 'a little' turns out to be an extra hundred thousand dollars a year, plus bonuses.

"I'm nervous."

"Don't be. You look amazing, by the way."

"Shut up."

"I need to give Sally a raise."

Sally is my personal trainer, which I've had for the last four months. When Lachlan suggested it, I told him that I hated gyms. But after a week with no job and nothing to do but paint, I decided to give it a try. After four months of consistent effort, it turns out I like being strong.

"Stop objectifying me," I say with a smirk.

"I can't help it. You know that."

I look across the sloping grass, and then turn to face Lachlan. "Hide me."

"What is it?"

"Damian. And like five of my friends." Ex-friends, I mean to say. It was only after Damian and I broke up that I saw that my entire social life was an offshoot of his. As I quickly found out, all my friends were actually *his* friends. It didn't take long for them to pick sides.

"Don't worry."

"Are they looking?"

He's silent for a few seconds. "No one's looking. And who cares if they do? They won't recognize you anyway."

He's right. Not only is my body different, but so is my hair. A month ago, after Lachlan told me how great I would look as a blonde, he paid for a hair appointment. With the new clothes, jewelry, and makeup, I don't look like the old Olivia anymore.

She was poor, overworked, and depressed. Whereas I'm rich, relaxed, and happy.

Still, I don't turn my head until we're around the corner. We're close to the lake now, walking alongside the dozens of runners and cyclists on Park Drive, all enjoying the still heat of the summer evening. Six months ago, I'd be at work at this time. On my days off, Damian would be dragging me to an underground art show, or arthouse film, or a dingy bar. He wasn't an outdoorsy kind of guy.

As we wait to cross over to the lake, I kiss him on the cheek, and then the mouth.

"What was that for?"

I don't reply, because the answer is too embarrassing to

say out loud. But I'm *happy*. Actually, genuinely happy. I know it won't last forever. I need to find my own career at some point. But as the months pass, I keep waiting for the other shoe to drop — and so far, it hasn't. Lachlan is still the same kind, generous, impossibly hot guy. And I don't feel like giving up my new life without a good reason.

He'll get tired of me eventually. I know that I'm just a fling. Though he's only a few years older than me, he's basically a sugar daddy. I'm sure most of the world sees our relationship like that.

He never treats me that way, though. In fact, he often tells me how much he wants a family — and I've realized that I want the same thing, before it gets too late. Damian had always scorned the idea of living a predictable suburban life. When I was with him, I figured we'd just be one of those bohemian New York couples that never had kids.

But as soon as Lachlan said he wanted a family, it was like something inside me unlocked. I felt a deep need to bring a child into my life. I actually wanted a family — and I wanted one with him.

It scares me, though, because there's another thing I want. Something that I can barely admit to myself, because I've never thought it would be possible.

I want to paint for a living. Not just as a hobby while I wait for Lachlan to come home, but for real. I want to exhibit my work. I want people to buy my paintings. I want to support myself — before I have kids and I run out of time. I've always been too nervous to admit that this is what I want. But with Lachlan, a new world has opened up.

"Where are we going?" I ask as we cross over to the boathouse restaurant.

"You'll see."

He takes me down to the water's edge, and while I watch him with a skeptical smile, he hires us a boat to take out on the lake.

"Really? Isn't this a bit touristy?"

"The Louvre is touristy, Olivia. The Grand Canyon is touristy."

"You're comparing this polluted body of water with the Grand Canyon?"

"Come on. It's romantic."

Soon, he's paddling us out into the middle of the lake. I look at the raised veins on his biceps, his strong forearms, and the question once more pops into my head: When will he tire of me? When will he trade me in for a younger model? Isn't that what men like Lachlan do? I'm just a dumb waitress, after all. Why would he choose me?

New York is full of beautiful women. For a man with Lachlan's looks and money, he can have his pick.

"You have to admit, it's beautiful out here."

"It's not bad. I mean, it's no Grand Canyon, but—"

He gestures for me to come closer, so I turn and lean against him. Despite my anxiety about when he will leave me, I feel warm and safe in his arms. I tell myself that it's fine. Even if it ends one day, even if he trades me in, I'll be OK.

"You have to paddle back, by the way."

I dig my elbow into his ribs. "Ass."

"Fine. Pass me that one, will you? Wait, look, there's something written on it."

I take the paddle on the left and see that someone has carved a sentence near the handle.

"*This is not a paddle.*" I raise my left eyebrow. "Really?

That's a lot of effort for a lame joke. I told you, I don't like Magritte."

"Tough crowd. Try the other one."

I roll my eyes and grab the other paddle. I stare at the sentence for what feels like a full minute, before turning to face him.

"Well?" he says. "You're making me nervous."

I glance back down at the paddle again, just to make sure I've read it correctly.

Olivia, will you marry me?

"You're the love of my life," he says. "And I want to spend the rest of it with you."

The old Olivia would be terrified. The old Olivia would want independence. The old Olivia would run away.

But I'm not the old Olivia anymore.

I say yes.

CHAPTER SEVEN

"Who's Yasmin?" I ask, as I pull back on my dress. "Did she own the house before you?"

I feel something brush against my leg and see Homer circle me, before leaping onto the pew to rub against my knuckle. Outside, I can hear the squeals of a child playing in the next-door garden. I glance at the window to make sure no one is looking at us over the fence.

"Not exactly."

Above my head, opposite the faded name, is a cross. Even though it feels like a desecration, I can see why he kept it. It's beautiful, ornate, and looks like it could be centuries old.

"Who is she then?"

"God, this is hard to explain."

"Just do it."

"She's my wife."

I feel my legs give out from under me. For the last six months, I'd been waiting for the other shoe to drop. This man is too handsome, too attentive, too intelligent to be with someone like me. I'm just an unemployed waitress, a failed artist, a loser.

And now, I can finally see why he treated me so well. He's a bigamist.

"That's a new one," I say. "Jeepers, Lachlan."

"No, not like that! I'm not still married. I mean, she passed away."

"You have a dead wife." I say the words as though I'm a language student hearing them for the first time. "Cancer?"

"No, she died in childbirth."

"Wow." I know I'm saying the wrong thing, but I'm not sure how to express my feelings at that moment. "How come you never told me about her?"

I have flashes of our wedding, which was only a week gone. It was just us and the minister at a church in North Carolina, overlooking the water. He told me that his parents were married there. I still hadn't told my mom about him, and he hadn't told his sister, so we did it alone. Somehow neither of us was ready to burst the bubble we had been living in for these last six months.

That night, we got drunk on champagne and he told me that his mother was the kindest and most beautiful person he'd ever known. He said his father could rot in hell, but his mother was an angel and he'd never forget her. He told me that I'd honored her memory, and that he felt like she was with us at the church, standing beside me, smiling with pride and joy.

I felt my love for Lachlan deepen that day. The fantasy was over. I began to feel like I was a real, permanent part of his life.

Avoiding my gaze, he looks up at her name in the chapel. "I knew those painters were going to half-ass the job."

"Lachlan! Please. We're married. That means you need to tell me about important things. Like being married. What else are you hiding? Are you a fugitive? Are you in witness protection? Do you have a bunch of kids?"

"I don't know." He walks over to the window, then smiles at my reaction. "Sorry, I do know about the kids. None of those yet. It's just, it feels like such a long time ago. And I didn't want to scare you away."

"I get it," I say, even though I don't. "But you didn't need to worry. You're deep into your thirties—"

"Not that deep," he protests, with a false laugh.

"You're ancient. Not that far off retirement—"

"Hey!"

"Honestly, it would be a massive red flag if you hadn't been in at least one serious relationship. But you should have told me. I'm in a little bit of shock."

He walks over to Homer and scratches his neck. He pretends to be fixated on making the cat purr, even though I know he'd rather we put him up for adoption back in Manhattan.

"I know, I know. But it felt different. It's not like we broke up. It might sound a little strange, but I didn't want you to be jealous of her."

I try to call Homer away, but Lachlan starts scratching him with both hands, and Homer just blinks at me before pushing his head even harder into Lachlan's fingers.

"How crazy would I be to feel jealous of a dead woman?"

"Not crazy at all."

"It sounds crazy to me," I insist. "You lived here with her? You bought this house together."

"After we married, we lived here for two years." He keeps his eyes fixed on Homer. "Until she passed away."

I feel a thousand more questions bouncing around in my mind, but his somber tone gives me pause. He's right. It is different. This isn't just his ex. This is someone he loved — and probably still loves. They never disliked each other. For all I knew, they never seriously fought. No one ever packed their stuff and said goodbye. They were about to have a kid together, for Christ's sake.

"I'm sorry," I manage.

"Don't be. Like I said, it's a long time ago. I'm over it." He looks up at last and touches my arm, and I can see the sadness in his eyes. "You're my wife now. My only wife. I love you."

As he walks away, all the questions leave my mind aside from one, which might as well be glowing neon above my head.

Do you love me as much as you loved her?

CHAPTER EIGHT

It's after nine when I wake, which means Lachlan's been gone for over four hours. Now that we live in the suburbs, he'll need to take an hour extra each day to commute, on top of his already crazy schedule. I won't see him much at all during the week.

But I can't complain. I have a gorgeous studio, a big house, a beautiful garden, and a husband. There's only one problem.

Her.

I take my phone from the dresser and search the web for her name. Yasmin Gibson. I didn't dare try this when Lachlan was home, but now that he's gone, I need to know.

But know *what* exactly? Do I want to see her face? Her posts on social networks? Videos? News stories about her death?

I scroll dozens of people that share her name, but none of them seem like a fit. I go deep into image search, social media profiles, and news sites. It's not until I hear Homer mewing at the door that I get up. Lachlan insisted that the cat stay out of our bedroom, and be locked inside the house at night.

"Poor guy," I say, tossing the phone aside. Maybe after someone dies, they eventually delete all traces of them from the web. Or do they leave social profiles active, so people can still like their posts, respond to comments, interact with their virtual ghosts?

Homer follows me downstairs, mewing and insistently bumping his head into my shins, until I empty a packet of cat food into his bowl in the laundry.

"There you go, buddy," I say, running my hand along his spine. "Must have been a bit scary to be in this big house by yourself. I couldn't sleep either. It's too quiet for me." I give him another scratch, then stand up. "Damn it, Olivia. You've been home alone for one morning, and you're already talking to the cat. Not a good sign."

I make a coffee, then wander slowly through the house. Lachlan gave me a tour yesterday, but I didn't get a chance to have a proper look. There are five bedrooms total, one of which Lachlan uses as an office. Three bathrooms, not including our ensuite. A chef's kitchen. A living room that's large enough to host a party.

I feel like a child walking through the house of an obscure older relative, unsure what I'm allowed to touch. It's like the house itself is judging me — and why shouldn't it? It's more sophisticated than I am. More expensive, too.

I want to believe this is my house, but I know it isn't.

Not yet.

It's still *hers*.

I stop in the living room, which has a dozen paintings, all clearly by the same artist. They're incredibly detailed landscapes from across New England. Hills, forests, meadows.

It's dusk in each, and there are no animals or other signs of life. Just empty landscapes before nightfall.

I go closer to the nearest painting to see who the artist is, but it's unsigned. I asked Lachlan last night, and he said he didn't know who painted them.

I take my coffee to the gate and check the mail, and see that they've given us a letter for next door. Sylvia Wood-house. An elderly lady, Lachlan had said. Though I know I'm being silly, I go inside and get changed — and even brush my teeth — before going to deliver it.

The house next door is smaller than ours, much more like a regular house, on a smaller lot. I think about depositing the letter in the mail, but decide that I might as well intro-duce myself. This wasn't something I ever did in New York, but growing up in Iowa I'd known the names of everyone on my street. We knew everyone's business — for better and often for worse.

I unlatch the gate and walk down a path to the front door. Before I can even knock, it's open. A tiny woman in a floral dress smiles up at me.

"Yes?"

"Hello, Mrs. Woodhouse. My name is Olivia Yates — I mean, Olivia Gibson. I've just moved in next door."

Her expression suddenly turns sour. "Gibson?"

"I have some mail for you. It was delivered to our house."

She looks at me like she's seen a ghost, then snatches the letter out of my hand.

"You've got a nerve," she hisses, then slams the door in my face.

I stand there for a moment, too shocked to move, before I realize that she's probably still standing in the hallway, watching me. As I turn to leave, I try to imagine what I've done to offend this woman — but the only thing I can think of is Lachlan. They probably had an argument about renovations or noise or the color of his house at some point, some stupid suburban disagreement, and it's carried over to me.

Stupid old bat.

When I get back home, I walk through the house into the garden. I put her out of my mind. I only have one job this morning — to paint. But as I approach the chapel, I hear an unusual sound coming from the fence, the opposite side to Mrs. Woodhouse. I go closer. It's the sound of a child crying. I can see a small wooden playhouse only a few feet away from the property line.

"Hello?" I call out, peering through the gap in the fence.

The crying immediately stops. A little blond boy pokes his head out of the playhouse. He stares at me, and after waiting a moment it's clear he's not going to say anything.

"I like your playhouse."

Nothing.

"I've just moved in. My name is Olivia. I like painting."

"My teacher is called Janet."

"Wow, OK. What's your name?"

"James."

He wipes his face and looks down at the grass.

"Why are you crying?"

"Mommy was being mean."

"I'm sorry to hear that, James. Why?"

"I hit her. And then kicked her." He pauses to wipe the snot from his nose. "And then I bit her."

"Poor Mommy. Did you think she tasted nice?" He cracks a smile, so I keep going. "Did you think she would taste like peanut butter? Or maybe chocolate? Or ice cream? Gosh, is your mommy made of ice cream? You're so lucky!"

I keep rambling on like this until he giggles.

"You're different."

"Different?"

"Than she was."

"Who?"

He looks above my head, at the house. "She's gone now."

Before I can ask another question, he walks away from the fence. He means Yasmin, presumably — but how would a kindergartener remember someone from so long ago? If it wasn't Yasmin, I suppose it might've been another girlfriend who lived here for a while. I want to call out after him, to ask questions about this woman, but I'm not ready to attract the wrath of yet another neighbor.

Instead, I go through to the chapel — the Sanctuary, as Lachlan called it — and begin to paint. Last night, I had come down and unpacked all my paintings from New York and arranged them around my easel. They're just pictures of still life, mostly potted plants and bowls of fruit. They aren't amazing, but in looking at them now I realize something new about myself, something Damian had always insisted wasn't true.

I'm good at this.

There are details in the pictures — the light on the table, the choice of color, the brush strokes — that feel true. That's new for me. I've never had the courage to paint the truth before.

But now that I have time and a place to work, the repressed creativity of the last decade, all that wasted time, is ready to come out. It feels wonderful, violent, alive.

It's only when I take a break that I realize my chest is tight. Underneath the excitement and joy of the work is a familiar feeling. Panic. I'm living my dream, but if Lachlan

has his way, that dream won't last very long. He wants kids —
and I want kids, too. But not yet. If I have kids now, I'll lose
my confidence. There's a chance I'll never paint again.

I need two years. By then, I'll be thirty-three. Will that
be too late? They say fertility falls off a cliff at thirty, but how
much worse could it really be? Even if I can get pregnant
then, it'll put a limit on how many we can have. One fewer
child, maybe two.

"Homer, what am I doing?" The cat blinks at me from
the altar, then turns around and licks himself. "Cryptic as
ever, Homes."

When I get up to the house for coffee, I see that the
supermarket has delivered groceries for the week. As I
unpack the shopping, I start making popping sounds with my
mouth, mimicking the opening credits of *Seinfeld*. I make a
mental note to stream the show tonight before Lachlan gets
home. This is one difference between me and Lachlan. He
hates television, especially comedies. Though he has a sense
of humor, he refuses to spend the few hours he has at night
on what he calls 'dulling his brain.'

I want to enrich my life, he would say.

I unpack the bag of Doritos I ordered and open them. I
don't know how Picasso did it, but for me the muse only
comes back when I bribe her with junk food. As I pour a
bowl of chips, I think about developing a serious reality TV
habit. I could binge one of those shows with beautiful, stupid
people cheating on each other. Something set on an island,
or in the south.

By the time I'm walking back to the Sanctuary — with a
half-finished bowl of chips and coffee number three — I'm
singing the theme song to *Friends* at the top of my lungs.

"I'll be there for you! When the rain starts to pour!"

I place my coffee on the table. Homer is stretching, probably preparing to stalk one of those endangered birds in the meadow. I make a mental note to research the collar, and then stare at my work from the morning.

Where do I begin?

And that's when I hear a voice from behind me.

"It's fall, actually."

CHAPTER NINE

I scream and drop my mug of coffee, which smashes on the chapel floor.

"Oh no, I'm so sorry!" A woman dressed entirely in black is jogging down the pews towards me. She crouches down and helps me collect the pieces of the shattered mug. I grab a spare drop sheet and use it to mop up the coffee, while the woman piles the pieces on a nearby pew.

"I'm Anya. Sorry, I'm a friend of Lachlan's." She stands and holds out her hand. She has a shock of disobedient dark hair that sticks out at random angles. "I thought I'd come and introduce you to the neighborhood. Didn't mean to surprise you."

I toss the drop sheet in the corner and shake her hand, feeling my cheeks go hot. "It's OK. Sorry you had to hear that. I think it might be what the kids call 'cringe.'"

"Your singing? No. It was like a nightingale."

I raise an eyebrow. "Really?"

"Well, a nightingale getting eaten alive by an eagle,

maybe." She laughs at her own joke. "Anyway, you got the words wrong. It's not pour, it's fall."

"What? I've heard that song a thousand times. Ten thousand maybe. It's definitely pour."

"Nope. Sorry, lady. You're wrong."

"No way."

She rubs her fingers against her thumb and tries to call over Homer, but he just stares like the Egyptian deity he resembles. "Way."

"If only some device connected us to all the world's information. Some sort of 'web' that would have the answer to our question."

"A 'net' maybe. Yes, that would help, but alas." She grins at me. "Agree to disagree?"

"Sure."

She goes towards the altar and looks at the stained-glass window. "This is so bizarre. Do you realize that this is a depiction of Jesus blessing a prostitute? Who makes that the central image of their church?"

"It's a bit different," I admit. A thought comes to me. "Hey, how did you get in? Was the gate open down the side of the house?"

"No." She smiles guiltily. "Sorry, I should confess. I actually know the code. I told you — I'm an old friend." I look away, wondering how many other friends Lachlan has given our security code to. "Don't worry, I only came down because I heard your voice. I wanted to meet you after hearing so much about you."

Though Lachlan would take me to parties and galas in New York, he didn't seem to have any close friends in the city. I had assumed he basically didn't have any outside of work. But maybe that isn't true. Maybe he'd left them all in

Rosford.

The thought that Lachlan might have a network of close friends that I need to charm makes me immediately nervous.

"He talks about me, does he?"

"He raves about you, darling." She squats down before the paintings I did in New York and examines them closely. "Where did you buy these?" she says, after a full minute has passed. "They have real promise."

"The canvas? That was in Manhattan."

"No," she says, looking confused. "The paintings. Who did them?"

"Uh, I did."

"Wow. Really?" She goes on her knees and gets even closer to the canvas. "The brushwork is very impressive. Where did you study?"

"Nowhere fancy."

"Secretive, huh?" She puts on the accent of a midcentury Hollywood agent. "Well, you've got talent, kid."

I can feel her eyes on me, so I look outside, desperate to change the subject. "It's very pretty here."

"Yeah, you can see right out to the meadow." She walks up to the window. "It was sad to see this place empty for so long. Lachie never let it go to seed, though. The gardener came every week. Even the cleaner came to keep the house ready. Just in case." She turns to me, smiling. "Expert deflection of a compliment, by the way. You'll fit right in around here. The people of Rosford are among the most emotionally stunted populations in the state."

Before I can respond, she reaches into her handbag and pulls out her phone. "Put your number in. We'll get coffee. Or something more original."

"More original?" I grin as I type my number into her phone and hand it back.

"Something stronger, maybe." She glances at the phone. "Gibson. You took his name? How retro."

I shrug off her comment. Taking his name had been a snap decision, and one that I had trouble explaining to other people — even myself.

"It meant a lot to Lachlan," I say. I look down at the coffee stains, the broken cup, and my unfinished picture. Though it's nice to meet someone friendly after old Mrs. Woodhouse from next door, I'm starting to wish Anya would leave. Sometimes this is all it takes to lose an entire day — just a single interruption.

"In for a penny, I guess. Oh, I shouldn't be so cynical. He believes in love. I suppose you do, too. Was I ever so naive?" She laughs, but notices that my response is cold. "Sorry, I'm divorced and never going back. This world is full of beauty, and love doesn't even crack my top ten. Art — that's all that matters to me now. Which is why I'm so excited to discover you."

"Er — thanks."

"Is it OK to say that? I know artists hate to think that way, but you need someone to help you, don't you? A champion? Not that I'm anyone so important. But I am the executive director of a gallery in town. I might be able to get you an exhibition."

"Really?"

"It's not solely my decision, of course. We have trustees that like to stick their beaks into our operations. But this work is strong." She types into her phone, and mine buzzes. "You should come to our next opening night at the gallery. I've texted you the details."

"Oh, no. I don't think so."

"Just think about it." She turns slowly in a circle, looking up at the rafters of the chapel. "I haven't been here in such a long time. Not since—"

She breaks off, giving me a cautious look.

"It's OK. I know all about her." I force a laugh and hope it sounds as casual as I intend. "In fact, I just saw her name painted on the top of the chapel. They've painted over it, but you can still see it in the right light."

Anya covers her mouth with her hand. "Oh no! Lachlan, you idiot. Honestly, men are so stupid about these things, aren't they?"

"It's fine," I say quickly. "It's funny."

"You have a different sense of humor than me, then. But you don't need to worry. He loves you more than anything." She glances at her watch. "And I love you, too. But I need to run. Walk me out."

I lead her out of the chapel into the garden. I plan to take her around the side of the house, but she heads to the back door.

Make yourself at home, I think, following her inside. I find myself giving her a half-baked tour, even though it's clear she knows the place better than I do. She pauses on the paintings in the living room, then turns to me.

"I love what you've done with the place," she says, a thin smile on her lips, and I decide not to correct her. "You've got great taste."

"Thanks," I say, opening the front door for her.

"Come to the opening!" she calls out, blowing me a kiss, before her black figure disappears through the front gate.

CHAPTER TEN

"Press the two buttons together to activate the oven."

I pause the video and follow the instructions. A light goes on and the oven begins to hum. That only took an hour to figure out, but hey — small victories. I pump my fist, then open my music app. I scroll past the obscure bands I had pretended to like for Damian and turn Taylor up as loud as it goes.

"Mew!" Homer curls around my ankles like a fat snake as I reach for a knife.

"Watch it, Homer," I say, dancing around the kitchen. I have a recipe open on my phone, and no less than 25 ingredients on the bench. "Let's do this."

An hour later, a chicken is in the oven, the vegetables are steamed, and I've sliced my hand in three different places. Unlike the dull knives I have at home, the Chef's Collection in Lachlan's kitchen cuts through everything like butter, including my own flesh. I've cleaned the blood from the tiled floors, though every time I try to do the dishes, the wounds open up, turning the water a shade of light pink.

While I wait, I dance to Taylor's greatest hits. She was always my secret love. I was supposed to be the art school girl, the cool waitress who only ever listened to obscure bands from Brooklyn. Now I wonder, was that all a lie? Was I always secretly craving to be a basic housewife, listening to pop music, and cooking overly complex meals to make my husband happy?

Maybe I'm both? But then, why just two people? Maybe I have the potential to be a thousand different people, and who I turn out to be just depends on the luck of the draw. After all, if Lachlan hadn't come to the restaurant that night, I'd still be in Brooklyn. And if Mom hadn't lost her mind, I might still be in Iowa.

Just as the timer is about to go off, I rush upstairs to get changed. I pick one of the dresses Lachlan has given me — fifteen at last count — and quickly apply some makeup. He likes a classic look, a red lipstick and eyeshadow, but I decide not to go the whole nine yards. It's best not to set a precedent.

When he arrives, I light the candles on the table and serve the meal. It doesn't look much like the picture in the recipe, but I'm proud of the work I've done.

"Ta da!" I say, as he comes into the dining room.

"Jesus, what's all this?"

"I thought you might like a home-cooked meal." He gives a tired smile, then comes across to kiss me. Up close, I can see dark circles under his eyes. "Are you OK?"

"Long day."

"Long drive?"

He seems confused by the question, then shakes his head. "No, I take the train, remember? Can I sit?"

While he pours himself a drink, I go into the kitchen

cabinet and take a Zoloft. I swallow it with water, and when I turn back to the table, I see Lachlan watching me.

"I wish you wouldn't take those."

"I need them. We've talked about this."

"I've heard they reduce your sex drive."

"Maybe I should sneak them into your dinner, then. Get myself a night off."

When he laughs, I feel strangely relieved. I sit at the table and cough.

"I was thinking about inviting Mom to visit."

"Mom?" He puts his fork down and touches his temple, as though the simple mention of family causes him a migraine. "I don't know, darling. We just moved in. And you don't even have a relationship with her."

"I know — but being here, in my new home, it makes me think more about family. Honestly, I feel terrible, babe. She didn't even come to our wedding. I feel like I owe her."

He picks up his fork and lets it hover over his plate. "From what I understand, she owes you more than anything."

"She doesn't have anyone," I insist.

"And neither did you! For fifteen years! Honestly, Olivia. Well and truly." He is silent for a moment, then takes a bite of chicken. "This is a little overcooked, darling."

That's a no, then, I think. I'm annoyed at his attitude, but I'm also relieved. Ever since I was a teenager, Mom and I have had a strained relationship. These days, she pretends to be some homespun midwestern housewife. I don't know what I hate more — the hypocrisy, or the fact that she was never like that with me when it mattered most. I could have used a mom twenty years ago. But maybe now I don't really need one.

"I never cooked much in New York," I say. "My kitchen was the size of this dining room table."

"Yes, but you're a grown-up now."

I scan his expression for a sign that this is a joke, but he's frowning. He's being a dick, but he's not wrong. I wasn't living like a grown-up in New York. I was working the same jobs I worked as a teenager in Iowa — and I wasn't even very good at them. I didn't know how to charm a customer or banter them into a bigger tip.

Now that I have some distance, it's clear that the only thing that kept me in those jobs was my looks. But I'm a wife now. It's not like I have to clean the house, or even do the laundry. A woman comes to do all that twice a week. All he really wants me to do is cook once in a while and look the part.

This is his world, and I've come into it willingly. I need to adapt. It's not much of a price to pay. I have a kind, handsome husband — and the time to paint.

"Your friend Anya came around," I say, changing the subject.

"Friend?" He shakes his head. "I barely know the woman."

"She said you were close."

"Not with me." The subtext is clear. She was friends with Yasmin. "Nosy woman in my experience."

"She was nice enough. She invited me to the art gallery."

"Oh?"

"I said no."

He raises one eyebrow. "That doesn't seem like a good idea. There's not many ways to get into this community, darling. If you had a baby, it's a different story. There are playgroups and all that. But for now, you have to make an effort. You'll be living the rest of your life here, after all."

The rest of my life? The turn of phrase causes me to jolt my hand into my glass of red wine. It spills onto the table and down onto my lap.

"Crap." I take a napkin and try to mop it up. "Oh no, it's on the dress."

"You stupid woman!" Lachlan stands up so quickly his chair falls to the floor behind him. From the kitchen, he tosses a roll of paper towels so that it lands on the floor beside me.

"I'll clean it," I say. I feel faint at the strength of his reaction — but also angry. "Jesus, what was that?"

"Jesus is right. That's one of a kind. I can't believe—"

Before he can finish his sentence, I take the roll of paper towels and storm out of the room, unable to stop myself from crying. In the bathroom, I take out my phone and search for how to get red wine out of a dress, but I can't read the instructions through my tears.

"What's wrong with you?" I whisper to myself, taking deep breaths. "He's been Prince Charming for six months, and his first bad mood causes a breakdown?" I stand up and look in the mirror. My makeup is smudged, so I take a wet wipe and clean it off. "Man. The. Eff. Up."

When I've calmed down, I go back into the kitchen. "We need vinegar and baking soda," I call out. "And one of us can get stain remover from the store. It'll be fine."

I expect to see him standing in the kitchen, looking bashful and ashamed. His reaction was objectively terrible, and I'm thinking I might get an apology. Maybe a kiss. Or maybe he'd take the chance to remove the dress and make love to me on the kitchen table.

But I don't get any of that. He's gone.

I walk through the house calling his name, but I can't see him anywhere. It's only when I go outside that I hear him. The basement is only accessible from the outside, and the door is slightly ajar.

Just like a man, I think. *Retreating to his cave when there's an argument.*

I'm about to go back inside and give him some space, when I pause. This is different. Because I don't hear the sounds of woodwork, or a pool table, or some other manly pursuit.

I hear him sobbing.

CHAPTER ELEVEN

I don't see Lachlan again that night, and he's gone before I wake up. I'm relieved to see from the wrinkle in the sheets that he slept in the same bed — it's a bit early in the piece for us to be having marital problems.

Still, I feel uneasy. If this were Damian, I'd curse him out and get on with my day. But I saw a different side of Lachlan last night. He was tired, impatient, and unkind. I want to say 'emotional,' but he's shown emotions before. If anything, he was *too* emotional before we got married — but the dominant emotion was his intense, overpowering love for me.

"No shit, Sherlock," I say, as I make my coffee. "He's a human being. He's allowed not to be perfect."

I hear the buzz of the doorbell. I swear under my breath and pray that it isn't Anya. I feel myself getting in the zone to paint, and I don't want her breaking the spell before it even begins. But when I open the door, a courier hands me a dozen white roses with a note inside.

I'm so sorry, darling. I'll make it up to you tonight xx.

I'm shocked by how much relief I feel. Last night, I was worried that this would become normal behavior. But the roses tell me that it is just a temporary blip.

As the courier leaves, I go to the mailbox and see that there's a note from the postal service. When I see the name, I almost drop the roses.

It's for Yasmin Gibson. It says she has mail to be picked up from the nearest post office. It's strange that she'd have mail after all this time, though I suppose not every business that has her address knows that she's dead. She's probably still getting email spam.

Our bodies are mortal, I think. *But in marketing databases, we live forever.*

I fold the note and put it in my back pocket, before taking my roses and coffee out to the chapel. While I wait for the caffeine to take effect, I sketch the roses. They're pretty, but also bland in their perfection. I try to capture this contradiction, but after an hour I realize it's going nowhere. I'd hoped the emotions of the night before would give my work some kind of charge, but now I just feel strangely *empty.*

I go into the garden and see the boy, James, hanging out by the playhouse. Without speaking, he sends some paper through the gap in the fence.

"What's this?" I ask, picking them up.

"I'm a really good artist," he announces.

"You are!" I say, looking at the pictures he has sent through. There's a tree, a cat, a child. And then a blonde woman standing next to the house with a cross on its roof.

"Is that me?"

He shakes his head.

"Is it the other woman? Is it Yasmin?"

He stares at me for a moment, then turns and runs away.

It's almost like the sound of her name has made him feel guilty, like he's coming close to admitting something he shouldn't.

My phone buzzes. Lachlan is asking how my morning is going. I scrawl out a text thanking him for the flowers, then go through my contact list. Since I left Damian, hardly anyone has texted me. I should just delete them all. When I get to Mom's number, I pause. I still feel guilty about not telling her about the marriage.

I try to tell myself that I keep forgetting, but the truth is, I don't want her to know because she'll disapprove. Everything about Lachlan is a slap in the face to my mother — his job in finance, his fast car, his suits, the excessively large house, his Ivy League education. Even his looks would be an affront to her. At Lachlan's age, every man in my home town is comfortably softening into middle age. For Mom, that's how it ought to be. That's how all the dads were in our town, strong but squishy, overweight, disheveled.

Whereas Lachlan in his work suits looks like he just stepped out of a fashion catalog.

The only thing that will help get Mom's approval is a baby — and I'm not ready for that. Not until I've seen how far I can go.

I put my phone away and get back to work.

———

I'M INTERRUPTED AGAIN before lunch by the gardener, a young, fit guy who says he'll be there a few hours, mowing the lawns and weeding the flowerbeds. I let him work while I make some food. The sound of the lawnmower is oddly relaxing. It's the sound I remember filling my hometown on the weekends. Every Saturday, dads across town would be outside getting their lawns to a respectable height before collapsing onto the couch with a beer.

Except for us. Our duplex didn't have a lawn — just a paved courtyard at the back. I didn't have a dad, either.

When I go back down to the Sanctuary after lunch, he's weeding the flower beds. His shirt is off and I can make out the knots of muscle in his lean back. He's an attractive boy. I wonder if he's been with any of the housewives in the area. That's a fantasy for some people, isn't it? To seduce the pool boy, gardener, the electrician? Or is that just a cliche from romance novels?

As he moves to cut the hedges, I turn my attention back to my painting. But before I can get started, I hear a voice behind me.

"I'm so sorry." I turn to see Lachlan standing behind me with another bunch of roses. "I was such an idiot last night."

"It's OK," I say, taking the roses and kissing him hello. "You already gave me roses, remember? These are nice, but you didn't have to."

"I don't know what's wrong with me."

"You're working too hard."

"It's worth it," he says. He kisses me again, and this time slips his tongue into my mouth.

"Watch yourself, tiger," I say, stepping back. "We have company."

He glances over my shoulder. "Right. I saw his truck parked on the street." He goes over to the door and leans outside, opens it. "Hey, buddy!"

The gardener turns his head and pops out his earbud. He walks over slowly. I pretend to myself that I don't take notice of his abs, glistening with sweat. "Yeah?"

"Take the rest of the day."

"You sure? They said I had to finish the whole garden. I got like two hours left."

"Don't worry, leave it." He reaches into his pocket and pulls out a few notes. "For your hard work."

"Alright." The kid takes the money and salutes, then goes back and hauls the sack of weeds out of sight — presumably down the side of the house. Lachlan goes out and helps him carry his tools and lawnmower on the next trip, and puts the ladder the kid was using to trim the trees down the far side of the house. When they're gone, I open the camera on my phone and use it as a mirror. I feel like wives aren't supposed to care how they look for their husbands, but I still want to maintain standards.

When he returns, I can tell what he wants to do. I spend a few minutes trying to convince him that we should go back into the house, but I can remember how it was the first time in the chapel, and I quickly give in.

Who knows, maybe I am developing a fetish for screwing in chapels?

Either way, we're soon naked on the mattress. I move it down a little, so I'm not looking at Yasmin's name, and let him lie on top of me. I finish just as quickly. It feels different this time — better, even — and he manages to finish at the same time.

It's only when it's over that I realize just *why* it felt different.

"Where is it?" I ask, as he turns away to dress himself, though I can already feel the answer to the question.

"What?"

"The condom."

"What?"

"Lachlan!" I move away from the damp patch on the mattress and pull my knees up to my chest. "You didn't?"

He's still not facing me. "I'm sorry. I got caught up in the moment."

"Don't lie to me!"

"I'm not! But is it such a bad thing?" He turns around to do up his buttons, clearly thinking he can argue his way out of it. "Don't you think it's time? We're married, we have a beautiful house, you don't have to work—"

I ball his underwear and throw it at his face. "This is my work. I'm not a Stepford Wife. I thought you knew that. My purpose in life doesn't revolve around helping you live out your fantasy. I'm a real person, Lachlan. You can't just make these decisions about my body."

"Of course, I didn't mean to do that. It's just that—"

I wait, daring him to say that I'm not getting any younger. He holds his tongue, but I know what he wants to say. And he's right, of course. We don't have long. I'm in my thirties now. My fertility, as Dr. Yang of Rosford Medical insisted on telling me, is falling off a cliff. There are two lives ahead of me. One as a painter, and one as a mother, and I want both of them. I want it all, just like Lachlan. He gets to have a family and a career, so why can't I?

When we're both dressed and inside, I grab the keys to the SUV. I know what I have to do, and I have limited time to do it.

"Where are you going?" he says.

"To the store. Your Stepford Wife needs to buy things for your dinner."

CHAPTER TWELVE

"Why do you need it?"

I'm standing in the Rosford drugstore — which, like everything else on the main street, doesn't seem to be a chain. The elderly pharmacist who is frowning down at me probably owns the place.

"Um—" I hear the rattle of the door, followed by the loud voices of two women. I wonder if I should have driven to the next town. It would be harder to explain my absence to Lachlan, but there'd be less chance of gossip. "I just need it. Usual reasons."

"This isn't candy," he says, typing into his computer. I wonder for a second if he's one of these pharmacists who likes to give moral lessons before refusing medications like Plan B. "Wait here."

A full minute goes by. I feel like a teenager buying condoms for the first time. I glance behind me at the women, who are standing in front of the cold medications. One of them has a stroller, which she moves back and forth like a vacuum cleaner.

"Here you go." I turn my attention back to the pharmacist, who slides the medication across the counter and rings me up. I hand over cash, because I don't want Lachlan seeing the transaction on our credit card.

"Can I have a bag, please?"

The man sighs and slides over a brown paper bag, leaving me to put the medication inside. As I walk back past the women, I can feel their eyes on me.

The main street is busy. It was hard to find a park, and it's just as hard to walk down the sidewalk without crashing into strollers. School must be out, and the town is packed with families — moms, some grandparents, packs of kids yelling and laughing.

This will be my life one day, I think, and it's not such a bad thought. Though the women are almost universally thin, and put more effort into their appearance than I'd like, the scene seems basically pleasant. The town is like a time machine, going back to an age of single-income households and mom-and-pop stores.

I find a deli and join the queue. There's a salmon pie in the cabinet, and I figure that will do for dinner. After I take Plan B, I probably won't feel like eating much, anyway. I feel a surge of anger at having to take it. Lachlan claimed it was an accident, but it wasn't like he was immediately overcome with passion. He helped the gardener carry his gear away, for Christ's sake. Just like the first time in the chapel, it was planned. That's probably why he came home early in the first place, to apologize, then have make-up sex.

It could happen to anyone, though. Right? It's a fact that guys hate condoms, and they'll always find excuses not to use them. He wasn't trying to trick me. He probably convinced himself in the heat of the moment that it didn't really matter.

If I was smart, I'd go on the pill again, though I always hated what that did to my brain. The doctor never told me about side effects when I first started taking it at sixteen, but when I came off it in my mid-twenties, it felt like I was suddenly a different person.

My phone buzzes and I see a text from Anya.

> Reminder: gallery Friday night. Come.

The text is quickly followed by another.

> Terrible paintings, good wine, great company (i.e. me).

I'm about to reply when I hear the women ahead of me talking conspiratorially. I realize it's the same women I saw in the drugstore. It sounds juicy, so I listen in while pretending to scroll on my phone.

"Can you believe it? The way she looks?"

"I know, it's creepy."

"That poor woman. She's barely cold in the grave and she swoops in."

"What about Lachlan, though?"

Lachlan. I almost drop my phone in shock. They're talking about me. I instantly blush. I turn around and pretend to be looking at one of the displays.

"He's grieving. He's not thinking straight. You know how much he loved her."

"Obsessed."

"Totally. If you ask me, she's taking complete advantage."

"Can you blame her, though? That house. My God."

"I knew he wasn't going to be single for long. But this isn't right."

"Creepy's definitely the word."

As I hear one of them place an order, I open the door to leave. The bell rings and I feel my face go hot. I tell myself to not look up as I pass by the front of the shop, but I can't help it. And just as I fear, the two women are both staring right at me.

As I walk back to the car, I wonder how many other people in this town already know who I am. How many people whisper as I walk by? How many of them already hate me?

CHAPTER THIRTEEN

"Wow. This is the art gallery?"

I'm standing in front of a building with a long glass frontage topped by thick slabs of stone. At one end, a tower rises up five or six stories. It's an astonishing building — especially given the size of the town.

"It's a Shawn Johnson. You know, the guy that did the Marble House out in Connecticut."

"You mean, one of the most famous architects of the last hundred years? He designed an art gallery for Rosford?" I let out a low whistle. "People in this town really wipe their asses with hundred-dollar bills, huh?"

"Present company excluded. That doesn't sound like the most comfortable experience. Anyway, it's not that big a deal." He opens the door for me, and I walk up the steps, my legs wobbling a little in the heels that Lachlan insisted I wear. "He was a local, I guess. Though I don't know how these things work. Maybe he has a team that does it and then puts his name on it."

I take Lachlan's arm and give his bicep a squeeze. "That's sacrilege."

"He's just a guy. That's the problem with you art people. You're always elevating these people into gods, then getting disappointed when the truth comes out. They're usually worse than the rest of us. Especially artists. They're always on the edge, mentally."

"That's a stereotype," I say, as we step into the gallery. "Besides, are you saying you want to send *me* away to the asylum?"

He gives a smile, which I read as condescending, though he's probably just reacting to the joke. Ever since I saw the other women in Rosford, I've been wondering if marrying me — the cool, poor, artsy girl from New York — was Lachlan's idea of rebellion. He was attracted to me because I wasn't one of *them*. He must be conflicted, though, because every one of his suggestions and gifts for me — the hair, the dresses, the heels — takes me closer to being a standard-issue Rosford wife.

Anya is standing by the entrance to the gallery. She kisses me and nods at Lachlan, before handing us both a flute of champagne. "You look stunning!" She pronounces it *stuh —ning*, and I'm almost ready to believe her. Today, Lachlan gave me the most beautiful dress I've ever seen. It's a vintage black Versace from the early nineties, and it fits me like it was designed just for my body. Without the personal trainer Lachlan paid for in New York, it would be literally bursting at the seams.

"This old thing?" I say, taking in her blue dress. "You look great, too."

"Please, you two make the rest of us look like peasants.

It's actually annoying." She loops her arm through mine and gives Lachlan a nod. "I'll take care of her."

Lachlan looks vaguely affronted. He gives me a kiss. "Stay out of trouble, OK?"

"Don't tell her what to do. Come."

Anya leads me through the crowd, pointing out various people from the community. The mayor, a squat woman with dark hair, is standing in the middle of the room, holding court. The principal of the local school. Two dentists. Three specialists at hospitals in New York. At first, I think she's just pointing out notable people, until I figure out that basically everyone in the room is notable. You can't afford to live in Rosford without being notable in some way.

I notice a few stares from the room, but with Anya I don't feel quite so worried about it. Who cares if people gossip? I feel like Anya will curse out anyone that's rude to me.

Lachlan is standing with a group of four other men, talking conspiratorially.

"They're all bankers. Two of them are Jack and Paddy, husbands of Paula and Helen. Helen works part-time at the gallery doing accounts, and Paula is on the board. Helen was at Goldman before she got married. They're both pricks, by the way. Jack and Paddy, I mean." She gives a guilty laugh and takes two more flutes of champagne from a circling waitress. She hands me one, forcing me to finish my current glass.

"This is a bit different from the boxed wine at openings I went to in Queens."

"I know. Rich people love to make donations to art galleries, even local ones. We actually have a surprisingly decent collection. But while I'm running this place, I'm committed to showing local artists. Hence." She waves her arm at the paintings on display.

I step closer and study the nearest piece. It's a beach scene, with a family of four eating ice cream cones next to a sand castle. There's a light surf, and the sky is blue. Though it's competently done, there's no tension to the scene, no purpose, no point of view.

"Not very good, is it?" Anya whispers.

I shake my head. "It's tired."

"Tell me more."

"There's no energy to it. I'm not sure why it exists. You can almost imagine the artist yawning halfway through. I mean, you could hang it in a coffee shop or something."

"Like to see you do better." I turn to see a dark-haired woman waving her finger at me. "It's easy to be a critic, isn't it, without getting in the ring for yourself?"

I'm too shocked to speak, and before I can respond, she storms off.

"Crap." I feel myself flushing while Anya laughs. "Was that—?"

"Paula Redstone. The artist we're celebrating today."

"Oh no. Oh no."

Anya takes another two glasses of champagne and leads me to seats in the corner of the room. "Don't worry about it," she says. "She needs to hear it. God knows I've said it to her face a thousand times. But like I said, she's on the board for this place, you know. Only reason we have to look at this pablum."

"She helps decide what goes on the walls here? Great."

"Don't be so sensitive."

As I sit down, I glance at Anya. She looks strangely satisfied by my exchange with Paula. Did she know Paula was standing right behind me? I feel like I'm a pawn in one of her games — but I'm still glad that she's on my side.

No one else is, as far as I can tell.

As I finish my second glass, I turn over some difficult questions in my mind, the ones I've wanted to ask Anya ever since I saw those two women in the deli.

"When did Yasmin—" I begin, but I'm interrupted by an angry voice.

"Excuse me, but Paula told me what you said." I turn to see a red-haired woman standing above me. She's maybe the same age as Anya, though without Anya's obviously Botoxed forehead and filled cheeks. Her voice is low and gravelly, like a smoker's. "I just wanted to say that was very cruel. Paula's incredibly nervous about this show."

I begin to apologize, but Anya cuts me off. "She told the truth, and you know it, Helen." I connect the dots and figure that Helen is the accountant Anya spoke about. "We all know it. That's why I didn't want this exhibition. People are laughing at her."

"The only people laughing are you two. This is a local gallery, Anya. It's not MoMA. If you want to be a snob, apply for a job down there. But this is for the community."

"Please. We need standards. This building doesn't exist to indulge the hobbies of rich ladies. It's an art gallery." Helen is about to respond, but Anya waves her hand dismissively. "Leave us alone. Honestly."

Helen glares at both of us, then storms off.

"Let's get out of here. I've got something to show you," Anya says. She stands up and swipes a bottle of champagne from a passing waiter, then waves me towards the door. I search for Lachlan, but can't see him in the crowd. "Don't worry about hubby. He'll be entertained. There's plenty of bankers in this room."

After a final glance through the crowd, I follow her down the hallway to the elevator. When we get inside, she hits the button for the top level.

"That's two enemies I've made tonight," I say. "Maybe I can insult the mayor and get the whole town to hate me."

"Please, you'd make more friends than enemies if you did that." She rolls her eyes. "Ignore her. She's just as bad as Paula. Honestly, these women are walking cliches. Their kids get older and they become absolute busybodies. Helen's been getting involved in the accounts for this place. Coming in late, auditing the books. Searching for a scandal. That's why I'm so glad you're around. At least you're real."

"Am I?" I mutter, absent-mindedly. "I actually thought she had a point."

"No you don't. You care as much as I do."

"I guess. I don't know."

"You *do* know," she insists, as the elevator door opens. We step onto a flat rooftop. The night is warm and still, and as I walk closer to the edge, I have a 360 view of the entire town. I touch the fence, which is only three feet high, and look down to a small courtyard below.

"Wow. This place is amazing!"

"Isn't it? We used it for exhibitions, but the health and safety people shut it down. Apparently you need more than a small fence to bring the public up here."

"So why don't you build a bigger fence?"

"It's a protected building. We can't change a thing from the original design without getting the historical society involved. Complete shitshow." We stand quietly for a moment, looking out over the town. I feel pleasantly lightheaded from the champagne, and it takes me a minute to remember what I wanted to ask.

"When did Yasmin die?" I blurt out.

Anya keeps her eyes fixed on the view. "Don't you want to have this conversation with Lachlan?"

"I don't want to bring it up. And I heard two women gossiping about me. They said something about her body being warm in the ground."

She swears, her face contorted like she's about to spit onto the polished floor. I suddenly imagine Anya as a rancher in the south, cursing at a wandering heifer, hocking into the dirt. I wonder suddenly if she was fated to have a different life, one better suited to her temperament and talents, but after a series of accidents ended up stuck in Rosford. She certainly didn't seem to particularly like anyone in town.

"Don't listen to them."

"Anya."

"Darling, it's not so recent. Eight months. If it was a divorce, no one would bat an eyelid."

Eight months. That meant Yasmin was almost literally warm in the ground when Lachlan and I first met. He would have been grieving then, and probably still is. "Not if we were dating, maybe. But we're married!"

"So what? It's romantic. And neither of you are spring chickens. It gets serious in your thirties. The clock starts ticking. And it ticks damn fast, believe me."

I know exactly what clock she is talking about. *My* clock. But that didn't make Yasmin's recent death any less squeamish. I want to ask more questions about Yasmin, but Anya takes my glass and fills it from the bottle of champagne, then uses the distraction to change the subject.

"So tell me. Where are all your works kept? I want to see them!"

"There aren't any," I say. "Nothing good, anyway. Ever since art school, I've just been... I don't know. Lost. It just hasn't happened."

"Art school? That must have been a decade ago! What the hell have you been doing?"

"I moved to New York, thinking that was the place to be. But the city was so expensive! I had to work insane hours just to make rent. And then there was my social life, and the fact that my room was a shoebox."

I'm talking fast, like a little kid explaining a fight to her parents.

"I was just tired all the time. There was no space for it. But I spent my twenties pretending that money doesn't matter, and then I turned thirty and realized it was everything. I told myself I had different values, but as you know, there's no art without money. I'm an embarrassment, really. A child can figure this out, it's so obvious, but apparently I needed an entire decade." I take a canapé from the tray and nibble its edges. "But meeting Lachlan really saved me. He changed my life."

"Yes, Lachlan's an angel," she says.

"Don't get the wrong idea. I love him, and I'd love him if he was poorer than me. He's kind, thoughtful and funny. But I love not having to work those crappy jobs. It's a godsend, Anya. I can do my life's work." I suddenly hear my own voice and stop talking. I never open up like this. But then, no one ever seems all that interested — and I'm not usually two wines down. "I'm sorry. Christ, I sound so pretentious. Can you tell I went to art school?"

She suddenly reaches across and grips my hand so hard

my knuckles crack. "Don't say that. You're different. You have real talent. Never forget that. In fact, I think you should have the next exhibition."

"What did you say?"

"You were right. This stuff doesn't have any life. But you — I can tell what you're capable of, Olivia. You just need to be pushed."

"I think you're the angel, not Lachlan," I say, stupidly. But I mean it. I'd rather have Anya's belief in my talent than polite friendships with all the gossiping idiots in town.

"Speak of the devil. Or angel."

Lachlan is standing above us, smiling.

"Darling, I didn't hear you come up here."

"I was looking everywhere." He turns to Anya. "Can I whisk her away? Some of us have work in the morning."

"Party pooper," Anya says, but she stands up and collects our empty glasses. "You're next, OK?"

Though I know I'll regret the commitment in the morning — I don't actually have any paintings worth exhibiting yet — I nod my assent and let Lachlan lead me away.

"Did you have a good time with your pals?" I ask, gently teasing, but he doesn't reply.

"You're drunk," he says, as soon as we get outside. "I thought we'd talked about this."

"What do you mean?"

"This is a small town, darling."

"What do you mean? I was with Anya the whole night." I'm puzzled, until I remember my incident with Paula and Helen. Maybe they complained to their husbands. I search for their names. "Did Paddy and Jim say something?"

"Jack. And we're having dinner with them tomorrow night, by the way, so it might be worth getting their names right."

"Wait, what? With Helen and Paula, too?"

"Correct." He opens the passenger seat, and I step clumsily inside. "It's important you get to know them."

"I don't want to know those—"

"Careful now. I've already booked the caterers that did the gallery, so you don't need to lift a finger."

"Hold on, it's at our house? You arranged a dinner party for tomorrow night at our house with two women that hate me?"

"Hush now. It's done."

"Lachlan, you can't!"

"I have to, darling. Jack and Paddy are very well connected. My firm isn't exactly thriving at the moment."

"I thought that was just the economy?"

"It's all just the economy," he says, with a booming, condescending laugh. "But firms come and go all the time. I need as many life rafts as possible. And relationships matter. That's why you need to make a real effort with Helen and Paula."

'Life rafts' seems dramatic. Our house is worth over three million, and we don't even have a mortgage. That's not to mention his other investments. So what if he loses his job on Wall Street? Why can't we just buy a normal house in a smaller, less fancy neighborhood? He could retire on what he's already made. We'd be just as happy. In fact, I'm certain I'd be more happy than in Rosford, but I don't tell him this.

I know that's not how it works. For people like Lachlan, there's always another mountain to climb.

"They hate me," I say. "I can't do this."

"We don't have a choice," he replies, with a sigh. "We don't have that kind of freedom, I'm afraid."

CHAPTER FOURTEEN

Next morning, I'm woken by the sound of a bell. As I unglue my eyes, I feel something pressing on my calf — Homer.

"What the—"

I see that the cat has a fat bell attached to its collar.

"Oh, Homer, what has he done to you?" I reach for him and try to undo the collar, but then decide to leave it. It's my cat and he should have talked to me first — but he's probably right. The meadow is full of rare birds, and I guess I don't want to be responsible for driving the yellow-spotted-whatever one step closer to extinction.

"It's a shame you're such an efficient killer, isn't it, baby?"

I scratch under Homer's chin and he presses closer, purring deeply. It's so easy to make him happy. If only it were that easy for the rest of us.

My tongue is scratchy, but my head is clear. On the drive home last night, Lachlan had made it seem like I was wasted, but I was never more than tipsy. A few glasses of champagne over the night — it's hardly a drinking problem.

Though as I make my coffee, I begin to wish I had actually been drunk. At least then I'd have an excuse for what I'd said about Paula's painting. It was a stupid thing to say at the opening night of her exhibition, and I didn't look forward to the apology I'd have to make later on. Anya might be able to fight these people, but I'm not used to having enemies. I'm the quiet, casually sarcastic girl, not the force of nature who insists on always telling it like it is.

And now, in less than eight hours, I need to entertain them.

It's not all bad, though. Anya has promised to show my paintings. But as I go into the Sanctuary, I know that I still haven't painted anything worth sharing. Honestly, all my paintings are just as lifeless as Paula's, even if the technique is marginally stronger.

I stare at the blank canvas for a few minutes, then decide to clean my brushes before getting started. I search for the turpentine, but see that the bottle is empty, so I go up to the house. I go through the cupboards in the bathroom and laundry, but can't find anything. I'm about to give up and drive into town when I remember the basement. The man cave. I've never been down there, but it's where I imagine Lachlan keeps his tools. There's bound to be some turpentine down there.

The door's locked, but I find a drawer full of junk in the living room. Underneath the junk mail and letters from the bank is a large metal ring with a dozen keys. Bingo. I try them all in the basement door until it clicks open.

I shine my phone torch down the stairs, expecting dust and spiders, but it seems remarkably clean. I search around until I find a light switch — then drop my phone in surprise.

It bounces down the stairs and lands on polished wooden floors.

This isn't an ordinary basement — it's been renovated into another room. There's couches and a wooden desk that was probably used a century ago for writing letters. In the corner on the near wall is a pile of boxes and a bookshelf. There's also a long rack of clothes wrapped in black plastic, and a set of dark wooden drawers.

On the far wall, there's an antique wooden credenza with a mirror and shelves.

As I get closer, I see why the basement was locked. And I also see why he was crying when he came down here a few days ago.

It wasn't because of our fight.

It was because of *her*.

The credenza is covered with photos of Yasmin, maybe thirty or forty, on every surface. Some are framed, others stuck to the wood with sellotape. The couch and two armchairs in the middle of the room are both set up to face the line of photographs. On the couch I see a pillow, a comforter, and a box of tissues.

This isn't a basement, I think. *It's a mausoleum. He lies on this couch, stares at the photos, and weeps.*

I take a closer look at the photos. The women in the shop said I was creepy, and I now see why. We're not identical, but I'm getting close. We have the same blonde hair, the same figure, the same skin tone.

A thought creeps into my head. Am I her replacement? Did he marry me to replace her?

Every new relationship is a replacement, isn't it? A new marriage necessarily replaces an old one — that's just how it works. And my connection with Lachlan is real. He hasn't been faking the last six months — no one could do that.

Still, it's clear that he's grieving for her, and that his grief is going to keep being a problem for our life together. If this really is my house now, I can't have a room remain dedicated to his dead wife.

This has all got to go.

Not just the stuff in the basement, either. There are three people in our relationship.

It's her or me. And I'm not going anywhere.

CHAPTER FIFTEEN

Before I know what I'm doing, I snatch a photo from the credenza and march back to the Sanctuary.

She's done everything before me. She's lived in this house. She's had her name painted in this chapel. She's slept with my husband.

A question pops into my head. Maybe it's the other way around. Am I sleeping with hers? Is she jealous of me?

Stupid questions. The woman's dead. There's no competition between us. So why do I still feel like she's here, watching me, taunting me?

I pin the photo to the side of my easel and begin to work. All the feelings inside of me — the resentment, the jealousy, the hate — come out onto the canvas. I paint through lunch, and by the time I'm finished, a likeness has come through. Not quite Yasmin, not quite me. Some third person.

It's good — better than the still life paintings I've done and a thousand times better than the drek Paula exhibited the night before.

Paula. I look at my watch and realize they'll be arriving

in less than an hour. But what about the painting? I can't leave it out for Lachlan to find. Stealing a photo of your husband's dead wife is creepy; painting her is creepier still. I'm not sure he'd be able to forgive me — not until he understood what I'm doing, anyway. And I'm not sure I understand that yet.

I pick up the painting and search the chapel for somewhere to hide it. Eventually Homer gives me an idea. Behind the altar where he sleeps is a small door, providing access to a storage area. I tug it open and gently place the painting inside. It's not exactly perfectly hidden, but there's also no reason for Lachlan to come snooping around.

I'll explain it to him soon, I tell myself.

But not until he's emptied the basement of all traces of Yasmin.

AS I GO INSIDE to take a shower, I feel giddy with excitement. I know I'm on the precipice of creating something real, and it eclipses any nerves I have for the dinner party.

A thought creeps into my head: What if I actually have talent?

What if I'm an artist *for real?*

I take my time in the shower, washing my hair and shaving my legs, and when I come out I can hear Lachlan downstairs. I want to confront him about the basement, but I have to keep getting ready before our guests arrive.

As I go into the bedroom, I see a dress laid out on the bed. Another gift. And next to it, a pair of diamond earrings. This must be his way of apologizing for the last-minute dinner. As I try on the dress — a stunning designer cocktail dress that must have cost a fortune — I decide to forgive him. These women are going to be in my life, whether I like it or not. And Lachlan's just a man. He doesn't really understand how delicate these relationships can be.

"You're cutting it fine," he says, as I come downstairs. Lachlan is bouncing on his heels, and it almost looks like he's nervous.

"Nice to see you, too." I smooth down my dress. "How do I look?"

He frowns at me, just as the doorbell rings. "You need to book an appointment at the salon. Your roots are showing."

"I'm growing it out," I say as he walks to the door.

"Not a chance."

Not a chance? I think I must have misheard him, but his expression suggests otherwise. He's in the same condescending mood as at dinner the other night. But as he opens the door, it's like a spell has broken, and his face lights up.

"Helen! Paddy!"

Helen comes in first and gives Lachlan a hug, before kissing me on the cheek. Paddy follows, a good head shorter than Helen, but thick and broad-shouldered like he spends too many hours in the gym. His beard scratches me on the cheek with his kiss, and his hand lingers on the small of my back. I have to consciously tell myself not to shudder or slap him away.

Lachlan leads Paddy into the kitchen to get a drink. The caterers are there already, putting together canapés.

"You look nervous," Helen says.

"I am nervous."

"The party is for you, isn't it?" she says, squinting.

"I don't know," I say, checking my makeup in the mirror. "But I'm never great at dinner parties."

That's not exactly true, because the fact is, I've never been to a dinner party like this. We didn't even have a proper dining table in our apartment in Queens, and none of our friends did, either.

Our friends. Damian's friends, more like. I still can't believe I let myself get sucked into his orbit for so long.

"Just give your opinions on house prices and the stock market and you'll do fine."

"Yikes. What if I don't have any?"

"Then it might be a long night." She gives a small shrug of her shoulders, then smiles as Lachlan comes back into the room with two margaritas. "Lachlan, you're a godsend."

"That's what I keep telling people."

"Which makes Olivia here an angel, I believe," Paddy says, coming up behind me. "You look ravishing."

"Put your tongue back in, for God's sake," Helen mutters.

An awkward silence follows. I can see a thin, ironic smile on Helen's lips. This is exactly what she wants.

A drama.

No. A bonfire.

"But you're right, of course. She looks amazing." She turns to Lachlan and touches his bicep, before throwing gasoline onto the flames. "And why wouldn't she? You've given her Yasmin's best dress. And her earrings, too!"

CHAPTER SIXTEEN

"How thrifty, Lachy," she continues, taking in my reaction before raising her eyebrow at Paddy. To his credit, he looks annoyed at this performance. But before anyone can respond, there's another knock at the door.

I glance at Lachlan for confirmation, but as he turns to the door, I immediately know that it's true. No wonder the women in town stared at me. I must seem like a crazy stalker that's trying to steal the life of a dead woman.

How could he do that to me? I try not to show the horror I feel, but I'm no actor, and Helen sees through my weak smile.

"They look amazing on you, though," Helen says quietly. "You have an amazing figure. Though, of course, Yas was something else." She turns to Paula, who is extracting herself from the clutches of Paddy. "You made it!"

"Of course!" Paula gives me a kiss on the cheek and a frosty smile. She looks around the living room. "I love what you've done with the place."

"Drink?" I ask, but before Paula can respond, Lachlan calls out his instructions.

"Get the girl to make another round of margaritas."

The girl. It was only a few months ago that I was *the girl*, the unnamed servant busting her ass for tips from people like this. I don't belong here, and they can all tell. I'm an imposter — a literal imposter thanks to Lachlan.

I give the order to the caterers milling in the kitchen, and then escape to the bathroom. I look in the mirror. What have I done to myself? Who is this woman? The only part of me I recognize is these uncertain, worried eyes. Despite the new body, clothes, and hair, I can't yet fake the easy confidence of the rich.

What would Yasmin do? How easy did she find these sorts of dinners? How effortlessly charming was she? How naturally beautiful?

I can't be her. But I can't be me, either. Not here.

There are tears forming in my eyes, which I dab away with a facecloth. When I'm calm, I go back out to the living room, where Lachlan is sitting next to Paula on the couch, with Jack perched next to her. Paddy and Helen are sitting in opposite armchairs. Two plates of blue cheese croquettes sit on the coffee table, untouched.

"I bet you can't keep your hands off each other," Paddy says, glancing at me as I come into the room. "I remember it well. The rush of being newly married." He lets out a vaguely sexual sigh. I see Helen roll her eyes.

"I certainly can't," Lachlan says.

"I bet Olivia can't either. She's certainly got a tight grip on you. Married in months! That must be a new record."

"We fell in love," he says. "Didn't we, darling?"

"Yes," I say, forcing a smile.

"You think you know everything," Paula says. "Love is only supposed to strike once. One person, forever. Isn't that true? And Lachlan has the most loving marriage I've ever seen." She pauses, and I can see the cruel glint in her eyes. This is her revenge for what I said last night. "When she dies, he falls in love again! Almost immediately! Who knew such things were possible?"

"Well, when you look like that in a dress, who can blame him?" Helen adds.

"Not me," Paddy says, flashing me a wink.

I look down at my feet, cursing the blush that is forming around my neck. I can feel them all staring at me, each with the same thought.

She seduced a poor, grieving man, and bewitched him into marriage. She tricked a vulnerable man, who loves her only for her looks. She's an empty vessel, a child.

I glance at Lachlan, who is frowning into his drink. I'm rescued by the caterers, who call us through to the dining room. I let the others go in first, but then realize my mistake. I haven't laid out seating arrangements.

"Male, female," Helen says. "And you're not allowed to sit next to your spouse."

"Helen!" Jack says. "This isn't your house.'

She glances at me. "Any objections?

"Well, I was thinking—"

"It's a great plan," Lachlan interjects. "Please sit, everyone."

There's a period of confusion as the group looks to enforce Helen's rules. I end up sandwiched between Paddy and Jack, facing Lachlan, who is laughing at a joke from Helen. I wonder if this is what she wanted — to be closer to my husband. Is that what dinner parties are in the suburbs?

An opportunity to flirt with — or even seduce — each other's spouses?

I feel hopelessly out of my depth.

"Cheers," Lachlan says, raising his glass of wine. I see there's one next to every plate. We lean in to clink glasses. As I meet Paddy's, he gives me yet another wink. "Dig in, everyone."

I look down at the artisanally crafted entree while Paula begins to talk about her kids. Helen does the same — they both have kids at the same high school — before turning her attention to Lachlan.

"Speaking of children, any news from your end?"

He smiles. "Not that I know of."

"She's drinking, Helen," Jack says. "That's a giveaway."

"Ah, the wine is non-alcoholic," Lachlan says, the smile still on his lips. "Just in case."

"You're joking," Paddy says, looking like he wants to be sick. "What's the point?"

"The point is that Olivia isn't left out, dummy," Helen replies.

"I'm not pregnant," I say. "You didn't need to do that."

"Just in case," Lachlan repeats. "We are trying, after all."

I feel my heart racing uncontrollably. Trying? Since when? I know I should keep my mouth shut in front of these people who will most likely spread gossip across town, but I can't help it. "No, we're not. Not yet."

"Darling," Lachlan begins, his voice slightly raised. His expression is the same one I saw when I spilled red wine on the expensive dress.

"We're not trying yet," I repeat, looking around the table. "One day. But we only just got married."

"Well, what about something you do agree on?" Paula

says, with a laugh. "What about the proposal? How did you do it, Lachlan?"

"Olivia can tell the story," he says. I can tell he's doing this to punish me. He knows that telling a detailed story to these people is the last thing I want to do.

"He took me out on one of those boats in the lake in Central Park. It was dusk. He had written the proposal on one of the paddles."

"That sounds pretty damn romantic," Jack says, raising his glass to Lachlan. "Well done. I didn't know you had it in you. I've never heard you be passionate about anything but forex transactions."

"Well, those are pretty sexy," Lachlan says, clinking his glass. "And it was romantic."

"Very," I add, glad that the tension has been broken. "I'm a lucky woman."

The waitress from the caterers comes through and spends the next few minutes taking away our entrees and replacing them with duck à l'orange, a dish I'd often served but never managed to try. I'm looking forward to eating quietly while the others talk about their kids or mortgages, when Helen giggles.

"Wait, I'm getting déjà vu," she says. "Lachlan, you're even thrifty with your romance. Isn't that exactly how you proposed to Yasmin?"

I freeze, just as I'm about to slice into the duck. I look at Lachlan for confirmation, and it's there, written on his face. "No," he says. "In New York, yes. But it wasn't the same."

"Ah, Yasmin told me differently."

"You must be mistaken," he insists.

Helen relents, a faint smile on her lips. She isn't mistaken — I can see that. Lachlan's special proposal wasn't special at all. It was used, second-hand, just like the dresses and the jewelry and the house.

Paula must guess that I'm suffering, but decides to keep the focus on me. "Olivia, we don't know much about you. Where are you from, again?"

She does know, but I can tell she gets a thrill from making me say it. It's amusing to her that I'm from Iowa — flyover country. They ask about the state fair and corn, and the levels of condescension are so high I feel like I might drown.

"I was actually closer to Chicago than the Dakotas," I say.

"And what did Mom and Dad do?"

This is critical information for them — a prime sorting mechanism. If they were lawyers and doctors, I'd go in one bucket. If they were teachers, another. I don't even know if they had a bucket for the truth from me, which is that Dad died in Iraq when I was a kid, and Mom was a receptionist.

"Raising two kids as a receptionist! That's heroic!"

"The cost of living in Iowa is so low, Helen," Paula explains. "They practically give away their homes."

This isn't true at all, but I don't bother correcting her. The mention of property prices soon leads to a discussion of investment properties and holiday homes. It seems like everyone has a large portfolio of property investments, including Lachlan.

As they complain about tenants, I excuse myself to go to the bathroom. When I return, the men are standing by the door.

"We're going outside," Lachlan says. I can see a cigar in his hand, and wonder for a moment if I've been teleported to a different century. The men go out to smoke cigars, while the women gossip in another room. The only thing missing is a billiard table. "The girls are in the living room."

As I go down the hall, I hear voices from inside and instinctively tiptoe to the door.

"Poor little girl," Paula is saying. "That was brutal. She doesn't even know what's going on here."

"I know," Helen replies in her distinctive, gravelly voice. "He's still grieving for her."

"Of course he is! I mean, it's a bit creepy what he's doing, but shouldn't she know better?"

"He's prince charming. Rich and handsome. Promises her a new life. Why wouldn't she take it?"

"You're not giving her much agency. I think she knows exactly what she's doing. I hope to God he doesn't have a baby before this ends. And it *is* going to end. Whenever the spell breaks."

I go back up the hall, then stomp back as loudly as I can. When I come inside, they're both smiling in my direction.

"Olivia! Join us!"

"Thank you so much," I manage, even though I want to strangle both of them. "But I've got a headache. If it's OK with you, I might go off to bed."

"Go, darling!" Helen says. "We'll take care of Lachy."

CHAPTER SEVENTEEN

"Is it true?"

I've been sitting on the edge of the bed for the last two hours, going through everything in my head. The basement, the proposal, the dresses — it all adds up to one thing. Helen and Paula are right. He's still grieving for Yasmin, and he's using me to somehow conjure her back into existence. I've been trying to think of a way out of this situation that doesn't involve a divorce, but I can't. There's no way we can stay together.

"Darling, I thought you'd be asleep. How's the head?"

"Is it true? Did you really propose to Yasmin in the same way?"

"Darling—" I can tell he's about to lie to me, but then he pauses. He points to the bed. "May I?"

"If you want."

He sits close to me, so I shuffle away to put some space between us. I don't want him touching me — not when he really wants to touch *her*. He doesn't talk for a moment, and I'm curious about what kind of tale he's going to spin, and not just about the proposal, but about all of it. Including the damn mausoleum in our basement.

"It's true," he says, finally. "It was the same as with Yasmin. Not exactly, of course. But Helen was right."

"Oh no, Lachlan." My heart sinks, and I realize how much I wanted him to have an excuse I could believe. For a second, I wish he'd lied to me — because how do we come back from this? "You're still in love with her."

"No!" he says. "It has nothing to do with Yasmin."

"Don't treat me like an idiot. I've had enough of that tonight."

"I'm not. Hear me out. I proposed to you there because it means something to me. Not because of Yasmin, but because of my parents." He looks down at his hands and exhales. "My father proposed to my mother there. They always used to talk about it. It's a tradition I wanted to keep. Yes, I did it with Yasmin first. But it's not about her. It's about my parents."

I scan his expression for hints that he's lying, but it looks like he's telling the truth. Still, I'm not ready to let him off the hook.

"What about the dresses? The earrings? Helen said they were Yasmin's."

"Not Yasmin's. My sister's. Yasmin used to borrow them."

"Your sister's."

"Yeah, she stores her stuff with me for when she's got events in New York. She used to stay when I was in the city. It's really not a big conspiracy. It's just an unfortunate coincidence."

"Unfortunate is right," I mutter. "And the blonde hair? That's just like Yasmin's, too."

"This is getting crazy, Olivia." He turns to face me. "How do you know what her hair color is, anyway?"

"This afternoon, I was looking for turpentine, so I went into the basement."

"Ah." He wipes his face with his hands. "This doesn't look good, does it?"

"No. It doesn't. What the hell is going on, Lachlan? Are you over this woman or not? Because you can't marry one person when you're in love with another."

Homer decides this is a good time to trot into the room. He leaps up between us on the bed, and begins to rub into Lachlan's knuckles. He scratches the cat's chin until he purrs.

"After Yasmin died, I couldn't deal with it. I had a breakdown, I guess. So I put all of her stuff in storage in the basement until I was ready to go through it all. But then I moved to New York because I couldn't stand to be here on my own, so I never got a chance."

I stroke Homer's back. "You have to get rid of it."

"I will."

"Now. I can't live here while you've got a shrine to her downstairs."

"I will. I just need to go through it all first."

"It's not that hard. Just hire movers and put it in storage somewhere else. Go through it there."

"Soon," he says, as Homer leaps onto his lap. "I promise. I love you. Only you."

"And the cat."

"He's growing on me."

"Literally, it seems."

"I'm good with pussy, er, cats." He gives Homer another scratch. "If you know what I mean."

"I'm trying extremely hard to not know what you mean."
I force a laugh, then stand up and let out a muted yell. "This
is so frustrating, Lachlan! I thought it was over, you know?"

"Over?" He pushes the cat away and I'm quickly
enveloped in his arms. "What are you talking about?"

"All the Yasmin stuff. And then I heard those two
women talking. They see it, too. They think I'm just a —
replacement, or something."

"Don't listen to them. Their lives are dull as ditchwater,
so they put all their energy into gossiping about the cool
kids."

"You think we're cool?"

"The coolest." He leans in to kiss me, and I let him.

"All the cool kids at my high school loved talking about
forex and real estate."

"Shut up." He kisses me more deeply this time. "I'm
sorry about the wine. I just really want to start a family with
you. And I thought, just in case, after the accident."

Ah, yes, the accident. He still doesn't know I took Plan B,
and I decide not to tell him.

"We have to talk about these things before you announce
them to the world."

"We will," he says. "I promise."

He kisses the top of my head and then pulls away.

"We still need to get your hair touched up."

"Lachlan!"

"It's up to you, obviously," he says, raising his hands
defensively. "But it's a judgmental town. It's just a helpful
piece of advice. You didn't like what Paula and Helen
said."

"Yeah, well, keep your advice to yourself."

While he brushes his teeth, I go downstairs to check the

kitchen. It's spotless — the caterers must have cleaned up after themselves. The fridge is full of leftovers.

I make herbal tea and take it outside. It's still warm, and there's a full moon lighting up the garden. The white Sanctuary almost looks like it's glowing. It wasn't such a crazy thing to put it here. If you're religious, why wouldn't you want to bring sacred places as close to your home as possible? Isn't that what we're all seeking? To get closer to something sacred, something real?

I walk over the grass and imagine Yasmin, standing in the darkness, painting. Gorgeous in her designer dress, her perfectly coiffed hair, her exquisitely toned form.

And as I imagine her, I'm consumed by hate. Despite what he says, she still haunts him.

I need to face the truth. I'm competing with a dead woman — and I'm losing.

CHAPTER EIGHTEEN

A month goes by. Every morning, I take a coffee down to the Sanctuary, pin the photo of Yasmin to the easel, and paint. While the weather is still nice, Lachlan spends Sunday mornings at his country club playing golf, so I have that time, too.

I'm now officially preparing for an exhibition. Anya texted me one afternoon that Helen liked the paintings from New York. Apparently Paula said I wasn't ready, but Anya flew off the handle, declaring that I was a genius and "too good for this shitty town."

I remember staring at the text message, paintbrush in hand, trying to remember what I'd be doing in my old life. Probably starting a new shift that would last for ten hours. I'd get hit on by at least two married men, and the head chef would brush past my ass half a dozen times over the course of the night. I'd end up with a few hundred dollars in tips — not bad, until it gets gobbled up by the insatiable demands of New York City rents and my student loans.

My life isn't the life of people with real jobs. It's the life of a rich housewife. Is that what I am now? My mother would kill me if that's what she thought. A waste of talent, she would say.

Screw that, I think, my paintbrush hovering over my tenth portrait. *This is real.*

When I take a break, I scroll through videos on social media. I feel a twang of guilt whenever I do this, because Lachlan is always talking about the ills of excessive social media use. For him, TV is bad enough for our attention spans; social media literally signals the decline of civilization.

But hey — sometimes I like to waste an hour or two watching videos of kittens interacting with infants. If that marks the decline of civilization, then sign me up.

As I'm staring at my phone, Lachlan texts. There are no words, just a link to an article about the risks of childbirth in older women. He sends these articles infrequently, even though I have a feeling he reads them all the time.

I draft back a passive-aggressive reply, delete it, then give a simple thumbs-up. There's no point arguing. We've reached a stalemate. Every time we have sex, he asks if he can skip protection; every time, I say no. It's wearing me down — but it's also keeping me focused on my work.

I can't waste any time. One day, I'll give in, and the real deadline will be set.

I go back to work, only to be soon interrupted by the gardener. We haven't had one since the shirtless boy came. It's been a relief to not have these interruptions, though the grass is getting wild, and I can see weeds poking through the rows of flowers.

I'm initially confused, because it's not the boy this time, but a woman.

"Who are you?" I ask.

She explains that she's from the agency. As I unlock the gate to the backyard she grins.

"I'll keep my shirt on, don't worry."

I remember how quickly Lachlan got rid of the guy when he came home. I thought he just wanted to have sex — but maybe he was also jealous.

"Wait, what did you say? Did someone call and complain because he wasn't wearing a shirt?"

She suddenly looks worried, and that's when I know the truth. Lachlan complained, and now we have a female gardener instead of a hot young guy.

"No, I don't know," she says. And before I can question her, she's striding towards the flowers.

I spend the rest of the afternoon trying to paint, but I'm distracted by the gardener, who keeps glancing in my direction and catching my eye. It's only when she leaves that I can get back into my flow. My latest piece shows Yasmin standing in this very spot, looking out at the meadow. She's less prominent in this picture, though I'm aware that she's the only thing giving the picture life.

"What are you working on?"

Shit. Lachlan — he's in the Sanctuary. I must have lost track of time. He's by the door, so he won't have seen it yet. I quickly take the photo from the easel and turn the picture around. I still haven't told him about my project, though he hasn't emptied the basement, either.

Another stalemate.

"I can't show you. It's not finished." I wipe my hands on my apron and walk towards him. "You're not allowed in here while I'm working."

"When's the show again?"

"End of the month."

"I can't wait to see it." He pulls me close and kisses me. He's in the mood, as usual. Lachlan has been ravenous — there's no other word for it. Aside from a few days when it was the wrong time of the month, he's been wanting me every night. I've managed to get him to every second night, but even this is a negotiation. Sometimes his intensity scares me. "Come inside."

"Alright, tiger. But let me tidy up first."

When I see that he's back in the house, I take the painting and place it in the cupboard. The rest are in there already, wrapped in plastic. I put her photo in there, too, then close the door and move my painting supplies to block it off.

Inside the house, I go straight to the shower and wash the paint from my body, then wrap myself in a towel. I find him in the living room.

"I'm going to get changed," I say.

He puts his hand on my side and shakes his head, then attempts to whip the towel from my body. He only succeeds in revealing my right boob, but the point is clear. We're not going to make it to the bedroom.

I soon find myself bent over the side of the couch, a pillow under my stomach and my head resting on a pile of cushions that he had already arranged there. I'm guessing he planned this, just like our times in the chapel. Another fantasy of his.

While he's in the bathroom afterwards, I extract myself from the position and get dressed. I can't complain. Eight months into our relationship, and he still wants me, even when there's no chance of a baby.

When I go to the bathroom after him, it feels different

than usual — but I see with relief that it isn't another 'accident.' He's tossed the condom in the bathroom trash, not bothering to hide it, like I usually do. Still, it doesn't feel right. He definitely wore the condom — but maybe it broke? Wrinkling my nose, I pick the thing up, rinse it in the sink, then fill it with water.

My worst fears are confirmed. There's a pinhole at the end, small and barely noticeable, but definitely big enough to cause me a major problem.

Why a pinhole, though? When condoms break, they don't leave tiny holes, do they? They burst open.

While Lachlan gets a drink of water, I go upstairs to the bedroom and open his bedside drawer. I take out a condom from the top packet and see that it's already been ripped open. I then tip the lot out, and find that they've *all* been opened.

I'm not ready to admit the worst, so I put them all back except one. I take it to the bathroom and give it the same test.

As the water shoots out of the pin-sized hole, I want to yell. I want to scream. But I know that if I accuse him of this, there's no way back. The stalemate would be over. Hell, the *marriage* might be over.

I wonder how many times we've done it with these faulty condoms.

Anyway, it can't happen again. I go to bed and instead of sleeping, I make a plan.

CHAPTER NINETEEN

"Just fill this out, please, Mrs. Gibson."

It's the next morning and I'm sitting in the Rosford doctor's office. There'd been a cancellation, so I'd managed to get an appointment with a female doctor on Saturday morning. Beforehand, I drove out to a strip mall ten miles out of town, where I got another round of Plan B and a new brand of condoms from a chain drugstore.

They would help — but the safest option would be to go back on the contraceptive pill. That way, if Lachlan had any more 'accidents' where he forgets to wear protection, I'll have another line of defense.

I copy over the details from my health insurance. This still feels new. In New York, I barely had any insurance at all, and any time I got sick I just prayed I wouldn't have to see the doctor. I'd usually go to the community clinic. The waiting room there was a depressing place, full of immigrant moms with kids in tow, drug addicts, the homeless.

This is where I am, I would think. *Only one rung above these people.*

But now, I'm not just one rung above them — I'm not even on the damn ladder anymore.

A few minutes later, a trim, older man comes into the waiting room. He looks to be in his sixties, though he's wiry and energetic, the type who runs marathons on his weekends. Dr. Yang. He's officially my doctor, though I'd specifically asked for a woman for this appointment.

"Mrs. Gibson. Lovely to see you again."

I hesitate. "Sorry, I was expecting—"

"Dr. Carpenter. Yes, we sometimes move appointments around. We're very busy."

The waiting room is empty. I think about making a new appointment — but I decide to go through with it. It's just the contraceptive pill, after all.

I follow him through to the examination room. He sits at a desk, types a few words into his computer, then turns to face me.

"What can I do for you?"

"I—I mean, my husband and I—"

"Lachlan."

I frown. "You know him?"

"I'm his doctor, too." His tone is condescending, all-knowing. "But I also know him from the club. He's a four, the lucky devil."

"Excuse me?"

He seems annoyed at the question. "Golf, Mrs. Gibson."

"Right. Well, anyway, we're not looking to conceive right now, so I was hoping — I mean, we need a prescription for the pill."

"What pill?"

"The, er, contraceptive pill."

He grunts, then types for a solid minute into the

computer. I can only assume he's creating a prescription, but when he turns back to face me, he looks angry.

"I'm afraid that won't be an option for you."

Not an option? "What?"

"I don't think it's a good idea. The contraceptive pill is fine for women who are in different situations, my dear."

My dear. I feel my heart begin to race. If I were a different person, I'd be demanding my rights, demanding a female doctor, demanding to be treated like an adult.

But I'm not a different person, and I don't do anything except look down at the carpet.

"Why not?" I manage, eventually.

"Family planning ought to involve the entire family. It's not for me to get involved in your marriage."

"It's my—" I begin, but he cuts me off.

"Yes, it's your body. But I don't like helping women go behind the backs of their husbands. Frankly, a woman your age—" He clicks the mouse on his computer a few times. "If you want a healthy family, you ought not to waste any time."

He types into his computer for what feels like an eternity. His printer hums, and he hands over a prescription.

"What's this?" I say, seeing the word Zoloft. It's the anti-anxiety medication I started taking back in New York. "I want the pill."

"Well, you won't get it from me. And you won't get it at my clinic. That should help calm you down. You wouldn't believe how many women come in needing scripts like this. Women like you, that don't need to work, that have cleaners and gardeners — and they're completely stressed out. Nothing to do, and completely hopeless. It's a very interesting phenomenon."

He stares at me for a moment, as if expecting me to

calmly discuss the mental health issues of local housewives. When I don't respond, he nods and gestures with his hand. The appointment is over. I can't bring myself to say thank you, so I just leave without saying a word.

I'm too shocked to be furious. It's only as I leave the office that I remember the only question I should have asked.

How does he know Lachlan wasn't involved in my decision?

CHAPTER TWENTY

When I get home, I find Lachlan in the kitchen making a veggie smoothie.

"Where have you been? I thought we were going out for brunch."

"Doctor."

"Zoloft?"

"Yeah." I'm glad he says it so I don't have to lie. I'm dying to tell him what Yang said, just to see him defend my honor against his golfing buddy, though I know I can't. "How did you know?"

He shrugs. "Why else would you go?"

"Anyway, the doctor said he knows you from the club. He says you shoot a four, whatever that means."

"It means I've spent too much of my life on the most infuriating game on the planet. It also means that the old doc is jealous. He can't sink a putt. Too much in his head." He switches on the blender for a few seconds, then unscrews the lid and sips the green potion inside. "I operate on instinct. It's what makes me great at my job."

"What is your job exactly?"

"Money."

I laugh. "You can explain it for real, you know."

"I know I can. And I have explained it to you about three thousand times at last count."

"Humor me."

"It's literally money. I buy and sell money. All around the world."

"And here I thought my painting had no societal value."

I expect him to laugh, but he just stares at me, a strange look on his face. "It's interesting. How does someone so intelligent have so little idea about how the world works? I could make the argument that moving money around *is* society."

"Please don't," I shoot back, and this time he cracks a smile.

"Fine. You win. I'm useless. We're both useless."

"At least we're hot." As I reach into the cupboard to find my bag of Doritos, I feel his hand on my ass.

"Hot is right."

"Cut it out. It hasn't even been twenty-four hours."

"Yeah, but aren't you ovulating? And doesn't that make you—"

"Oh my God, I *so* regret telling you about ovulation." I run my hand along the back of the cupboard but still can't find anything. "Where's my snacks?"

"You're an addict." He presses himself against me and kisses the back of my neck. "But I can help you get clean."

I push against him and get myself free. "Lachlan! This is serious."

"No it isn't," he says with a laugh. "They're gone."

"What?"

"I threw them out."

I can't believe what I'm hearing. "You did what?"

"They're not healthy. If we're going to have a baby, you need to eat better. No processed foods. Cut down on sodium. I was going to get rid of the coffee, too, honestly, but—"

"You didn't!" I don't know what to do, so I stomp the floor like a child.

"I left the coffee. But I did buy you folate tablets. It's a little late, but take them now and they should have some effect. Did you talk to Yang about it?"

Yang. It takes me a second to realize that he's talking about Doctor Yang, his buddy from the country club. "No! I told you, that's not why I was there! And Lachlan, I haven't agreed to this yet. I'm not ready."

"You feel ready to me." He steps closer and touches my waist with his hand. I can't believe it. After this conversation, he still thinks he's getting action.

I slap his hand away. "I'm not."

"OK. I get it." He's looking at me thoughtfully, as if I'm some awkward South Pacific currency that isn't appreciating in value quite as he expected. "But can you at least take the folate? Just in case you're ready in a few months."

"No! No folate. And no sex. Christ, it's like being married to a fifteen-year-old. You're a horny old goat."

"Technically, I think that would make me a horny young goat."

"A goat either way." I dodge his embrace one more time and head for the door. "Stop. I have a hair appointment."

"Whereabouts?" He looks pleased, and I'm not surprised. He's been dropping hints about my roots for a while now.

"Maggie's."

"Have fun," he says. "I'll miss you."

MY APPOINTMENT IS at a small salon in town. I'm greeted by a girl who looks no more than sixteen, though I've long found it impossible to judge the ages of young people.

"Mrs. Gibson, welcome. My name is Mia. What are we doing today?"

There are a few other customers inside, but thankfully none of them take any notice of me. And after today, hopefully the comments will stop.

"I want to color my hair. Brunette."

She studies my hair for a moment, then nods. "Warm?"

Warm? Does that mean light? I have no idea, so I just nod.

"We can do that," she says.

After washing my hair, she takes a call at reception, then gets to work. While she goes through the motions, I read a murder mystery on my e-reader set in the Scottish highlands, which isn't very gripping but has the effect of making me want to travel. That's another thing I won't be able to do if I get pregnant. I'll be Rosford-bound for years, especially if Lachlan insists on a large family, which I have every suspicion he might. Even if I object, I can see Lachlan slowly chipping away, until I wake up one day, forty, pregnant, caring for four kids under ten.

It wouldn't be such a bad life. But it wouldn't be *my* life.

After letting the color set for forty-five minutes, Mia leads me to the sink and washes it out. We're walking back to get it styled when I see what's happened.

My hair — it isn't brunette at all. It's blonde. I'd been too wrapped up in my book to see what she was doing.

"What the hell is this?" My voice is raised. I see other customers watching me in the mirror. "This isn't the color I asked for!"

"Mrs. Gibson, please."

"What?"

"Your husband rang up and said—"

"My husband?" First the doctor's office, now the hair salon. Is my body even *mine* anymore?

"Mr. Gibson. He did it before. It's a surprise. With—"

She trails off, but I quickly realize what she's saying. Lachlan used to tell the hairdressers what to do with Yasmin's hair. And so they assumed he'd be able to do it to mine.

"My husband doesn't get to decide my hair color." I'm glaring at Mia, and the poor girl is almost in tears. I can tell this scene is going to get her in trouble with her boss. But I don't care. I'm not letting him win, especially not after this morning.

"I'm sorry."

"Do it again," I say, putting on my best impression of an entitled rich lady. I pray that this girl doesn't see how fragile this confidence is, how little she would have to push back before I'd give in. I only wish I was capable of this same confidence with Dr. Yang, and not just a teenage hairdresser. "Brunette."

"It's not great for the hair—"

"Again. And do what I asked, this time."

CHAPTER TWENTY-ONE

"I think I need to get a divorce."

I'm parked outside our house, running the air conditioning in the summer heat. It's a Saturday afternoon in the summertime, but the street is empty. Growing up in Iowa, a street like this would be packed on the weekends with kids riding their bikes, playing tag, drawing on the sidewalk with chalk. Here, kids have activities, schedules. They're all reverse-engineering their lives towards an optimal college application.

"Don't be stupid. He was being romantic, if you think about it." I can hear Anya half-cover the mouth of her phone to yell at her son. "The man wants kids and wants you to be beautiful. I know it's a little 1952 of him, but not every woman would complain."

"I feel violated."

"Don't exaggerate. In terms of the protection, he's probably worried that it might not even happen. It's a little controlling, maybe. But he's a stable man that wants kids,

Olivia! Do you know how rare that is? You found the one! You should be doing everything you can to keep him."

I'm staring at the house across the street, and it's only when Anya stops talking that I realize it's staring back. Two black cameras poke out from the top of the garage like the eyes of an alien.

"That's depressing."

"Look, you know I have no love for Lachlan. He's a controlling asshole. But on the spectrum of available men, he's about as good as it gets. You know I'm right."

I give a grunt of annoyance, but it's true. The only other long-term relationship I've ever had was Damian, and he used to leave bruises across my body. Lachlan's never come close to that. He's charming, kind, handsome. Rich.

I hate to admit it, but even if Lachlan wasn't quite so kind or charming, I'd find it hard to leave for another reason — the time I have to paint. To lose that time every morning would be like cutting off a limb.

"I don't mean to be harsh, but you've got to think about what you're bringing to the table here. You've won the lottery, and now you're complaining. If I were you, I'd pop out a bunch of kids, hire a nanny, and live your life."

"OK," I say, to cut her off. "Thanks for the pep talk."

"Anytime. Now, when can I see your paintings?"

"Soon. Soon. See you."

After she finally hangs up, I pull into the driveway. I'm still furious about the salon, but when I walk inside the front door, I'm also nervous. Because there's no way I can let this go without a conversation. And I'm not sure how that's going to end. He clearly thought I'd roll over — like I've rolled over about everything else. The clothes and jewelry, the basement, the condoms, all the not-so-subtle attempts to force me to have a kid. He's stepped over the line — and now we have to bring everything to the surface.

"Lachlan?"

"Upstairs!"

I don't want to say anything I'll regret, though if he pushes back too hard, then I know all my suppressed rage is going to spill out.

"Where are you?"

"In our room."

When I open the door, I can hear him in the ensuite. There's a folder on the bed, and when I get closer, I see that it's from a travel agency. I didn't even know those still existed. Intrigued, I open it and find brochures to hotels across all the major European capitals.

And beneath all of them, an itinerary.

"What is this?" I ask when he comes into the room.

He walks up to me, smiling his charming smile. "You look beautiful."

"What?" The words don't add up. I feel like I'm back in New York, staring at some experimental painting, searching for meaning that never comes.

"That's our honeymoon."

I look back down at the itinerary. It's a month-long tour across the continent, starting next week.

"My show."

"I'm so sorry. But it's the only time I'll have in the next twelve months. I've been negotiating this for ages. But you'll be able to go to every art gallery and museum in Europe. And maybe I'll get to take you to the opera once in a while."

"Lachlan." I don't know what to say. It still doesn't add up. Just a few minutes ago, I thought we were heading for a divorce. "The hair—"

"I crossed a line. I'm sorry, OK? I just think you look hot as a blonde."

"You can't control me like that."

"It was supposed to be a surprise."

"How would you like it if I gave you a buzz cut without your consent?"

"I'd be the coolest kid in finance. I might even get some respect from the Harvard bros I'm supposed to supervise."

"Please."

He touches me on the hip. My body betrays me. I feel warmth spreading through my chest.

"This trip. I can't believe it."

"I know Rosford can be a little claustrophobic. But we have the whole world in front of us. It's bigger than we can imagine."

"You told me that once before," I say. "It was a very seductive line. Back then."

"What about now?"

I can see that I'm going to have trouble fending him off. "One second."

I go downstairs to the kitchen to get a glass of water and then text Anya.

> Bad news. I have to cancel the exhibition.

Anya's response comes back within ten seconds.

> What?? Helen is going to flip.

> Going on honeymoon to Europe. Do you think I'll be able to postpone it to another date?

Leave it with me.

It's disappointing, but I have to play the long game. A month away would give me a chance to truly solidify our marriage — and escape from the ghost of Yasmin, once and for all. When we come back, he'll finally be ready to empty the basement, and we could make a fresh start.

I hear his footsteps behind me, and put away my phone.

"Can I touch you now?" he asks.

"On one condition."

"Anything," he moans, as he cups my ass with both hands.

"Give me one year before we have kids."

I'm genuinely curious about the way he'll say no. Lachlan likes to control everything.

"Give?" he says, with a smile. "What's there to give? We need to agree on that decision."

"Do you mean it?"

He forces a laugh, though I can tell he's getting annoyed. "I can't get anything right today, can I? Let me try again. I don't want to have kids for a year." He suddenly gets down on his knees and begins to plead. "Please, Olivia! I'll do anything! No children!"

He pulls so hard at my hands that I fall down on top of him. We're soon making out on the spotless marble tiles. As my clothes come off, I try to force myself to be in the mood.

He's an alpha, I tell myself. *He's used to being in control. I'll just have to set some boundaries.*

"I suppose I need a condom, don't I?" He gets up on his knees. "I'll go and get one."

"No, don't." I reach across to my bag, which I'd tossed onto the kitchen floor when I got home. I fumble inside, then toss him one from the pack I had purchased at the pharmacy. "I didn't like those ones. I got these instead."

As he kneels above me and tears it open, he gives me a look, and that's when I know the truth. He did it — he intentionally put holes in our condoms. I try to keep my face blank, but I'm no actor, and when he pushes roughly inside me, I wonder: Does he know that I know?

And if he does, where does that leave our marriage?

CHAPTER TWENTY-TWO

I could barely sleep that night, and in the morning I skip painting for the first time in a month to research European art galleries.

Living in New York had been one thing. But the capitals of Europe were on another level entirely.

The Louvre.

The National Gallery.

The Rijksmuseum.

Picasso. Monet. Manet. Miro. Van Gogh.

The list goes on.

I'm still buzzing when I hear a knock at the door. I figure it's a courier delivery, and I let out a loud "oh!" when I see Helen standing on my doorstep.

"Sorry to intrude."

She's wearing a designer sundress with Dior sunglasses pushed up above her forehead. Despite the heat, she looks cool, composed, and — as always — expensive. For a second, I have the bizarre thought that maybe rich people don't sweat as much as the rest of us. Their bodies are trim from private trainers, their clothes are made from more expensive materials, and everywhere they go is perfectly air conditioned.

I hesitate for a moment as she looks past me expectantly.

"Come in," I manage.

"Thank you." As she steps inside, I admire the waves of her red hair. "I'm sorry to come unannounced. I would say I was just in the neighborhood, but I suppose I always am."

I force a smile. "Would you like a drink?"

"Please. Water."

I walk to the kitchen, expecting her to follow, but instead she stays in the living room, staring at the paintings on the wall. I can't blame her — they are extraordinary — though when I come back and give her the water, I can't help but feel like a waitress again. I wonder if this is exactly the response she wants from me.

"I could look at these forever."

"Yes, they're beautiful," I reply.

"I'm not sure that's the word I'd use," she says, turning towards me. "They're fascinating. And not just because of what happened. I think they're sinister."

I keep looking at the paintings, and realize that she's right. There's something off about the vivid colors of the scene, their unnatural scale, their sheen. It's as if the pictures have mutated away from beauty into something cruel and unnatural.

"She was a talent, wasn't she?" Helen continues. "What are the odds? Two talented artists occupy this house, one after the other. You could almost say he has a type."

My chest suddenly feels tight. I step away from the paintings as if they could sting me. "What do you mean?

Who are you talking about?" The look of pity on her face makes me want to scream. "Yasmin?"

She gives a small nod, and then walks over to the coffee table and places her glass of water on the coaster. "I thought you knew. How could you not?" She gestures to the room, full of perfectly selected antiques. "This is all her. You think Lachlan has this taste?"

How could I not know? Yes, what sort of idiot assumes that her husband wouldn't leave paintings by his ex-wife on the wall of their living room? What sort of idiot assumes that marriage is a clean slate? What sort of idiot assumes that she won't have to compete with a dead woman?

If I am competing, then all the evidence so far says that I'm losing badly.

I feel Helen's eyes on me, and I try to compose myself. "Please, have a seat."

She frowns slightly as she goes to the couch, the same look of pretend-concern on her face. "I'm sorry. I've upset you. I actually came here to find out why you've canceled your exhibition. It's very late in the piece. We're not going to be able to find a replacement, you know."

I sit across from her and force a smile. In five minutes, I'll pretend that I have a dentist's appointment and get this interfering woman out of my house.

"Lachlan surprised me with a trip."

"Yes, I heard. A honeymoon. How romantic. I was just wondering — did it have to be at the same time? Couldn't he move it?"

"It's his work," I say. "It's so cut-throat over there. He says this is the only time."

"What nonsense. Our friend Geoffrey who works with Lachlan is taking time off the following month." She sits with the pregnant silence for a beat too long. I stand up. Every sentence out of this woman's throat seems designed to wound me — and drive a wedge into my marriage. As if reading my thoughts, she breaks the silence. "Where are you going?"

I rattle off the list of cities in order. Paris. Barcelona. Munich. Athens. Rome. I expect her to give platitudes about the beauty of Europe, or perhaps some dull anecdote about her own honeymoon. But instead, she just looks down at her hands and frowns.

"What is it?" I ask

"It sounds like a marvelous trip." She abruptly stands up and moves towards the door. "I should go. I'm so sorry."

"Helen, did you come here just to make me feel bad about the exhibition? It's really quite pathetic. The gossip in this town is unbelievable. Don't you have a life of your own?"

"Yes, I do." She suddenly looks exhausted, her composure lost. "I might as well tell you. No good you finding out when you're already there. It's exactly the same trip."

"What are you talking about?"

"The honeymoon. It's the same one he took with Yasmin."

CHAPTER TWENTY-THREE

The same proposal.

The same house.

The same decor.

The same paintings on the wall.

The same hair. The same clothes. The same jewelry.

And now, the same honeymoon.

I can't take it anymore. It's like I've been cast in someone else's life. I'm wearing her costume, speaking her lines, screwing her husband.

But it's all still *hers*.

When I first heard about Yasmin, I worried she would haunt me like a ghost. But I'm not being haunted; I'm being transformed.

I keep all this to myself, my reaction muted until I get Helen outside, because I don't want to give her anything else to gossip about. But as soon as Helen leaves, I race upstairs to find our shared laptop. I open the tickets he forwarded me, and then click through to the airline.

It doesn't take me long to cancel them. They're nonrefundable, but I don't care. I then go through all the hotels and cancel them, too.

A trip of a lifetime, gone. But it wasn't the trip of my lifetime. It was the trip of *her* lifetime.

It doesn't take long for Lachlan to call. He tries three times, before sending a text.

> What have you done?

> I'm not going on Yasmin's honeymoon.

After that, he doesn't reply. And what could he say? If he denies it, I can just ask Paula, or Anya, or anyone else in town that seems to know everything about Yasmin and Lachlan's perfect little marriage.

While I wait for him to get home, I take Yasmin's paintings off the walls and move them down to the basement. Even though I resent her, I'm careful with them. Helen was right; they are extraordinary. She was an enormous talent.

When I'm done, I text Anya, Helen, and Paula in a group and tell them the show is back on. Anya texts back privately to ask about the honeymoon, but I don't respond.

I EXPECT him to rush home early, but he doesn't get back till after seven. I'm sitting in the living room, nursing my second glass of wine.

Divorce.

The word sits in the back of my throat. I force myself to say it out loud.

"Divorce."

I take another sip of wine, then attempt the full sentence.

"I want a divorce."

Is that what I really want? No — but if he doesn't think it's a real possibility, then this shit is going to continue forever. Next week, he'll be apologizing because we eat the meals that Yasmin liked to eat; then, the music she liked to listen to. He'll eventually be booking me in for surgery to make my nose like hers, then my chin, and my eyes.

When we have kids, he'll probably name them after her family.

I don't want a divorce, but what choice do I have? Everyone has their limits, and these are mine. Anya said I won the lottery. She said I should be grateful. But I'm not really trapped here. I can build a new life on my own. I might even get enough in a divorce to start again.

When he finally arrives, he's carrying a bunch of roses.

"I'm so sorry, darling," he says, rushing towards me. When I don't stand, he hovers for a moment, before sitting next to me on the couch. "It was an accident."

"You must think I'm stupid." I'm looking ahead, at where a TV would be in a normal house.

"No, no, I don't. It was just... the travel agent had organized this trip before. And I'd thought you'd love it."

"I'm not her. I don't want to copy her life, you know."

"You're being ridiculous." He leans back and rubs his eyes. "These are the major cities in Europe. It's what everyone does."

"Not everyone. Her."

"This is insane. You don't need to worry about her. She's dead, Olivia."

"Do you know that? Do you accept that? Lachlan, I'm not Yasmin. I will never be Yasmin."

"I know that! Don't you think I know?" He looks so

anguished that I almost feel sorry for him. What if he's right? Those cities are typical of an American touring Europe. "This is just a coincidence. Seriously. I didn't even think about it."

"What about the hotels?" I ask. "Are those the same, too?"

For a moment, he doesn't respond, and I see the truth. All my suspicions, confirmed. He wants to use me to recreate the honeymoon he took with his dead wife. But at the look of regret on his face, my anger softens, and I'm reminded of what's driving his behavior.

He's not trying to hurt me; he's just grieving for Yasmin. Despite myself, I feel sympathy for him.

"This is sick, Lachlan. If this is going to work, you need to accept me. You can't just force me to be like her. Because I'm not."

"It wasn't like that. Honestly, I was just being lazy. It was such a great trip. I wanted it to be amazing for you, and I knew you'd love it." He puts his arm around me. "I'm sorry. Seriously."

He tries to kiss me, but I pull away and make an excuse that I need to go to the bathroom. I sit on the toilet seat and let myself cry.

I can either go back and accept his lies and go on like normal, or I can realize that it's never going to change, and leave. It's not really a choice. He's not ready to be married. He's still consumed by grief for this woman. It's going to be the hardest thing I've ever had to do, but it's not my job to put up with it.

My marriage is over.

"Divorce," I whisper to myself.

I just need to say it out loud, once, and it will be done.

When I'm finished crying, I search in the drawers for tissues, but there's a pile of junk — old toothbrushes, Lachlan's shaving stuff, my pads.

Pads. I glance at my phone. Late, but it's only been two days. Surely it's not—

I go through the rest of the drawers until I find the test. I unpeel the plastic, then take the little stick and follow the instructions. I remember the drawer of condoms. I took Plan B twice, but what about all the other times we used faulty condoms? But I'm only two days late. It happens all the time.

It doesn't mean anything, I tell myself.

Except this time, it does. The results are clear.

I'm pregnant.

CHAPTER TWENTY-FOUR

Pregnant. What does that mean?

Forty weeks till this is done. Forty weeks till my life is entirely taken by another creature.

Lachlan did this to me. He *forced* this on me. He ruined this moment, which should be the happiest and most fulfilling time of my life. Because it's not my moment anymore. It's *his*. It's his victory. Despite everything I told him, he managed to do what he wanted with my body.

This means I have forty weeks to do my life's work. After that, I'll need to transform into Helen and Paula and do my best to raise a child in this strange, privileged world. I'll always be an outsider here, but my child will have all the privileges of this community. Private schools, private hospitals, music lessons, ski vacations — everything that I never had.

I try to imagine their entire life, to force myself to feel love and pride. To force myself to want it to happen.

Even though what I really feel is blind panic.

Forty weeks. My career, such as it ever was, will be done.

I won't be an aspiring artist anymore. I'll be a mom. A housewife.

Forty weeks.

Let's make the most of it then.

I keep the news to myself and the next morning, I take my biggest canvas — six by eight feet — and place it on the floor. I paint like a maniac, entirely on instinct. I don't look once at Yasmin's image, which remains clipped on the easel.

When I step back from the painting a few hours later, I see that the woman I've painted is myself. The younger me, just before I left Iowa. Surrounding me is a swirl of color. What does this mean? Anya would probably say it's the existential void or something. But to me, it's showing the possibilities in front of me, the blank slate of my life at that point, the sheer possibility of it all.

Before I know it, I'm crying. That girl is gone now. She's as dead as Yasmin. All the details in my life have been filled in, all the choices already taken.

I'm trapped. Lachlan trapped me.

All I can do is get used to it.

FOR THE NEXT TWO WEEKS, I paint like a woman possessed. I keep the photo of Yasmin with me at all times, and the hatred and resentment I feel for this dead woman flows into my work.

We're together, her and me. A permanent connection.

I'm working ridiculously quickly, but I'm certain every finished work is the best thing I've ever done.

At the end of every session, I feel like I've been diving

underwater. When I come up for air, the world is different — simpler, sharper, and for a time, easier to live in.

As I finish each piece, I pile it in the cupboard in the chapel. Soon, I'll be showing them to the world. But not the world, really — just the notable people of Rosford, Lachlan, Anya. The busybodies Helen and Paula. Each work feels like a betrayal of Lachlan. But they're also true. And I can't waste a single brushstroke on a lie.

Lachlan and I continue as if nothing has happened. The condoms, Yasmin's crap in the basement, his ongoing, unprocessed grief, the honeymoon — it's all buried deep. It's like when art historians X-ray famous paintings and find, beneath the picture on top, something entirely different. Something unseen that somehow changes the meaning of everything on the surface.

With every day that passes, I know that I'm another day closer to blowing it all up. Because when he sees these paintings, he's not going to think of me as the cute, pliable waitress anymore. Who knows? He might want to divorce me.

But it'll be too late.

Because I'm having his baby.

ON THE DAY before the show, I wake up early to bring out all the paintings I've completed. The delivery van comes just after eight. I keep a watchful eye on the guys carrying the paintings, and follow them to the gallery to make sure they're all unloaded carefully.

Helen meets me there and guides me to the storage area. When the paintings are all unloaded, Helen walks slowly down the line, before turning to me, a small wrinkle in her forehead.

"You've got it."

"Huh?"

"Anya was right. I don't know if genius is the right word. But this is courageous." She comes close to me and takes my hand. "Are you sure you want to do this?"

I knew then that she saw Yasmin in the paintings — and that meant everyone else would too, including Lachlan.

"Speak of the devil."

"I don't think I'm the devil in this situation," Anya says. She's leaning against the doorframe, shaking her head slowly. "Olivia, can I have a word with you?"

I follow her upstairs into a small office overlooking the car park. She sits me down on a small sofa. "You can't do this."

"What are you talking about?" I'm physically jolted by her reaction. Even if there's only one person who understands my work, I thought it would be Anya.

"It's not worth it."

"It's not that bad."

"You've painted his dead wife!"

"I had to." I'm aware of how stupid the words sound against the truth of her accusation. "It was the truth."

"The truth! Well, here's another truth. He's going to divorce you. I mean it. This is humiliating."

I shake my head. "He won't do it."

"What makes you say that?"

"He just won't," I say, placing my hand on my stomach. I hold her gaze until she understands.

"Christ, he got his way, did he? You guys really know

how to bring the drama." She lets out a low whistle. "I can't convince you to kill the exhibition, can I?"

I shake my head.

"Then good luck. You're either brave or stupid, and my money's on both."

As she opens the door to leave, I call out after her. "Hey, Anya?"

"What?"

"Are they good?"

She turns around to face me, and shakes her head like I'm a toddler that's just finished finger-painting the walls.

"You're talented, dedicated, and extremely brave, and that's the best definition of genius I know. But that's not a compliment, Olivia. It's going to bring you a world of trouble."

CHAPTER TWENTY-FIVE

When I get home, it's just gone nine. I change into my jeans, then make coffee. While I'm waiting for it to brew, I feel a scrap of paper in my pocket, which turns out to be the letter from the postal service.

Yasmin's letters — I forgot to give the paper to Lachlan.

As I drink my coffee, I look up the process for getting access to a dead person's mail. It says that I need proof that I have legal authority to manage her estate, which requires letters testamentary or letters of administration. And then I'd need a death certificate and ID.

I don't have any of that. I don't totally even know what it all means. But why does it matter? The letters are none of my business. They're probably just spam, anyway. Who even sends letters these days?

But this is different. It's a PO box that's been closed because Yasmin stopped paying the bills. Why would Yasmin have a PO box? There's probably an innocent reason. But I have to kill time until the exhibition tomorrow, and I need something to distract me from the creature growing in my stomach.

But there's one possible way for me to get access to her mail. I find the key in the drawer and go outside to open the basement door. After I switch on the light, I see that nothing has changed. Even the photos of Yasmin are still stuck to the credenza.

I march to the other side of the room and begin searching through Yasmin's desk. In the third drawer, I find what I'm looking for.

Yasmin's driver's license. It's still valid for another month. Perfect.

Before I leave, I go to the boxes lined up against the wall. The first box is full of old books — thrillers, mostly, along with a tattered copy of *Jane Eyre*. I lift it off, then look into the second box. More books. I'm about to put the box back when I spot a pile of photos tucked down the side, held together with a rubber band.

As I take a look, I swear under my breath.

They're nudes. Hundreds of them. At first, I wonder if the photos are of me, but then I see that these are of my doppelganger.

It's Yasmin, taken from what must be hidden cameras in the house. There's Yasmin in the bathroom, looking in the mirror. And in the bedroom, pulling on her underwear. There's a few dozen of these before Lachlan makes his first appearance. I know I shouldn't look, but the compulsion is too strong. There are photos of them kissing. Undressing each other. Giving each other head. There's even pictures of them having sex throughout the house, including the kitchen.

I pause on the images, wondering why they seem so

familiar, until I realize that *we've* done all these places and positions, too. Every one of them is a carbon copy of what Lachlan and I did together.

In the last photo, he's taking her from behind and staring right at the camera.

Right at me.

CHAPTER TWENTY-SIX

It's like a spell has been broken. I know, all at once, that my marriage is over. The life I had planned — the still mornings of painting, the beautiful house, even the happy routines of marriage — will never happen. It's burned up, like a roll of old film.

I think of all the times we had sex in unusual places. The mattress in the Sanctuary. The living room. The kitchen floor. He must have taken stills of me, too. They're probably sitting on his computer somewhere.

I feel the presence of Yasmin. He did this to her. He spied on her. He controlled her.

But not me. Not anymore.

While I'm still in the basement, I go online and call a dozen movers until I find a company who can come that afternoon.

While I wait, I go inside and try to see where the cameras are hidden. I make sure to have an excuse to be in every room, so he doesn't get suspicious. Remembering the angles of the photographs in the basement, I find them hidden in the smoke alarms in the bedroom, kitchen, and living room. There's another one in the light fixture in the bathroom.

He's been watching me this entire time. I imagine him sitting in his office at work, watching me shower, watching me get changed, watching me dance to pop music.

I long to give him the finger and rip them out, but I still have work to do. I go to my room and pile all the designer dresses he has given me on the bed, and take photos of each one. Within an hour, I've listed them all online. If I get the right price, I should end up with thousands of dollars, if not tens of thousands.

I then take all the jewelry he has given me and put it in a small bag. When I have the chance, I'll drive to a jeweler in another town and have it valued. And then I'll sell the lot — even my wedding ring. Even if I don't get any money in the divorce, that should give me enough money to set myself up somewhere else.

An hour later, the movers arrive and begin taking away all the stuff from the basement. I stand in the driveway, watching them work.

"What's going on?" I look down to see the little boy who lives next door coming up from the garden. "Are you moving?"

"How did you get here?" He ignores the question, but I can't help but think about the times that Lachlan and I had sex in the Sanctuary. "Do you come through often?"

"I used to come over and play with the lady who used to live here."

I feel strangely jealous to think of Yasmin bonding with this little boy. "Was she nice?"

"Yeah. She said strange things though. Mom says she was crazy and I wasn't allowed to come over anymore."

"Why? What did she do?"

Before he can respond, one of the movers yells out.

"We're done," the driver says. "What should we do with it?"

"Like I said. Sell it all."

"And the proceeds, so to speak?"

"Text me. I'll pick it up. You get half."

He gives me a mock salute. "Pleasure doing business, lady."

I turn around and look for the kid, but he's gone — probably scrambling over the back fence, even though it seems much too high for him to climb.

When the movers are gone, I peer into the basement. It's completely empty. I feel light, like I've set Yasmin free from her prison.

I'll soon be free myself. Soon, but not yet.

I take out my phone, and within a few seconds, I find the number online.

"This is Family Planning Services. How may I help you?"

I can feel the sun on my legs. The sweat running down my ribs. My eyes suddenly wet with tears.

This is my body, I think. *Mine.*

He forced this baby on me. If I have it, I'll never be free. He'll always be there. He'll have lawyers that get him visitation rights. Co-parenting. I'll have to stay close, dependent on his child support just to stay afloat.

"I want to book an appointment, please."

"Yes? To see the doctor? What kind of appointment?

I look directly into the sun until my eyes hurt. This isn't what I want, but it's what has to happen. Because of what he did to me. He'll never control me again.

"I want to terminate a pregnancy."

CHAPTER TWENTY-SEVEN

The closest appointment was next Monday. To distract myself, I drive to the post office to pick up Yasmin's mail.

As I wait in line, I study the ID. I'm a brunette now, but even without the change in hair color, we still look eerily similar. No wonder Lachlan chased me so hard in those early days. I must have seemed like a ghost walking into that restaurant.

The ghost of Yasmin.

"Next."

I slide over the letter Yasmin had been sent.

"Yasmin Gibson?"

"That's me." I hand him Yasmin's ID. "Sorry for leaving it so long. I've been overseas."

"That's OK."

She glances at the ID, then at me, then places it next to her computer and begins typing furiously. I glance up at the cameras. I'm committing a serious crime. Mail fraud, identity theft, false representation — any one of them could land me in prison for years.

But who's going to care? Yasmin's dead, and Lachlan probably doesn't even know this PO box exists.

"You want to close down the account?"

"Yes, please."

I give her a few more details, then sign a form — and it's done. She slides over a single envelope, attached to a receipt with a fat rubber band.

"Thank you," I mutter. As I leave the post office, I take one more glance at the camera looking down at me. I feel like a bank robber after a successful heist.

When I get to the car, I immediately pull off the rubber band and check the address. To my surprise, it isn't addressed to Yasmin at all. The name on the front is Alex Khoury.

Khoury — that was Yasmin's maiden name.

Next to it, scrawled in capitals with red pen: RETURN TO SENDER.

The return address is the PO box. The letter is clearly from Yasmin to someone in her family. These are Yasmin's words. I consider ripping it open there in the parking lot, but that feels disrespectful. The words of a dead woman are sacred, and need to be respected.

I carefully fold the envelope and put it in the pocket of my jeans.

After the show, I tell myself. *After I've left Lachlan, once and for all.*

WHEN I GET HOME, I'm half-expecting to find Lachlan already there, ready to fight. But the house is empty. I have the rest of the afternoon before I need to get ready for opening night, so I go down to the Sanctuary. I find Homer lying on the altar, his eyes half-closed.

"Don't get too comfortable," I whisper to him. "We're leaving tonight."

I choose a small canvas — one of the few I have left — and begin to paint. It initially feels like a self-portrait, but halfway through I realize that it's someone else.

Not me. And not Yasmin, either.

It's a third figure, another uncanny replica of Yasmin. It's only after a few hours of work that I see what I've done. It's Lachlan's next wife, the one that is sure to replace me after I leave. But there's something different about her. The expression is fixed, the eyes glazed.

I step back and gasp at my own work. She's dead. I've painted a corpse.

When I go inside to clean up, my chest feels tight. I clench my stomach as I feel the familiar waves of adrenaline hit my nervous system.

Anxiety, my old friend.

I can't feel like this — I have too much to do. I go upstairs and take a CBD gummy from the back of my drawer, then take a Zoloft. I forgot to take it this morning, so I do exactly what the doctor warned against, and take two at once.

What's the worst that can happen?

But just as I finish the thought, the world suddenly tilts up towards me, like I'm on a ride at a theme park. I fall onto the bed in a heap, and everything goes black.

CHAPTER TWENTY-EIGHT

I wake to darkness and a splitting headache. My tongue feels like a slab of sandpaper in my mouth, and I'm worried if I move my lips they'll split open.

I sit up and discover that I'm no longer in my clothes from the morning, but one of Yasmin's old dresses. It's tight around my hips and I have to swivel on the bed to get up.

I feel my hair fall against my back. It's wet. *Oh no.* I switch on the lamp and walk to the mirror to see what he's done. My brunette hair is gone — he's dyed it back to the platinum blonde he likes. I'm wearing jewelry, too — a necklace, a bracelet, two rings. He's even done my makeup, though it's a little smeared from the pillow. There are heels by the bed, waiting for me to step into.

I've been drugged. Lachlan must have seen me empty the basement on his cameras. When I was at the post office, he could have come back to the house and swapped out my pills.

He drugged me. And all for this. So that I would look like *her* again.

Yasmin. The love of his life.

I look to the bed and see that the pile of dresses I had arranged for sale has disappeared, too, along with the bag of jewelry. I open the closest — they're not there either.

Of course he knew. He has cameras in every room. Who's to say he doesn't track my internet usage, too? I open my phone to check the listings, and sure enough, they've all been taken down. He must have logged all my passwords.

Nothing I've done since I've been here has been a secret. Nothing except my painting. The camera in there must have been focused on the place where we had sex, and not where I worked.

Small mercies. I go into the bathroom and drink from the tap until my tongue stops feeling like sandpaper, then take two aspirin. God knows how they'll react with everything else in my system, but I know I need to think clearly.

As I stare at myself in the mirror, I try to remember what I looked like — not just before I met Lachlan, but before I moved to New York City, over a decade ago. What happened to that young woman, that girl? She thought she would move to the city and find herself. But I see now that I've been faking it the whole time. Every step of the way, I've let other people define me. Not just Damian and Lachlan, but my professors at college, my boss at the restaurants, my so-called friends. I've always twisted myself to fit their expectations.

Not anymore.

I search in the cabinet until I find a pair of scissors. *I should almost thank you, Lachlan,* I think, as I take a length of my hair and chop it free. *Never again will anyone tell me how to live.*

An hour later, my head is completely shaved. I find my

jeans on the floor and put them on, along with my favorite paint-splattered hooded sweatshirt.

Perfect.

I then stand on top of the toilet to reach the light fixture. There it is — the little black camera. There's a small wire running into the ceiling. I pull it as hard as I can, and it snaps off.

One down.

I find a stepladder in the garage and go through the rest of the house, giving each camera the finger before snapping it off. Soon I have a small pile of twisted wires. They look like the legs of an enormous insect.

I'm about to throw them away, when I pause. It must be illegal to record someone in their home without their permission, even if it's your spouse. I could go to the police with this. Get him thrown in jail. With whatever drug is in my system, there'll be enough evidence to put him away for *something*.

But despite it all, I don't want him locked away. Just a few weeks ago, I was in love with this man; to my shame and confusion, those feelings still haven't disappeared. I don't want to hurt him.

I just want to be free.

I thought I could make this work. I thought that Lachlan was a normal grieving husband. But there's nothing normal about this. He doesn't want a new wife. He wants his old one back — and he won't take no for an answer.

I look down at the Sanctuary and mourn the life that I never really had. A life with time for dedicated, meaningful work. Is that too much to ask?

The answer, I see now, is obviously *yes*. But it doesn't matter. If I stay any longer, Lachlan will start forcing me to walk like Yasmin, talk like Yasmin. Soon enough I'll lose myself for good.

I'm about to leave when I remember my last painting. I can't leave without it. I'd left it to dry in the Sanctuary.

I run downstairs, praying that he hasn't found it, but then I smell the smoke. It's too late. The Sanctuary door is wide open, swaying in the warm breeze, and to the left, still smoldering, are the ashes of my latest painting.

I let myself stand there for a few minutes, mourning the destruction of my work. But he hasn't beaten me. I can paint it again. There's nothing he can do to stop me.

I feel a rush of excitement about the work I'll be able to complete once I'm free. All I need to do is get through the show, then I'll pack my things and leave.

Before I go to the car, I look at myself in the mirror. I don't look like Yasmin anymore, but I don't look like myself, either. This is someone new.

I can't wait to meet her.

CHAPTER TWENTY-NINE

The gallery is full.

Though I know it's not just because of me — this is basically a party for people in town — I feel a rush of fear and pride.

There must be a hundred people here. And they've come to see my paintings.

They've come to see *me*.

I walk slowly for a minute through the crowd until I spot a familiar presence marching in my direction.

"You've got balls." Paula looks me up and down as I stand next to her. "This is something else."

I take an orange juice from a circling waitress. "Thanks."

"It's not a compliment. How could you? That's—" She lowers her voice so that the man next to us can't hear. "Yasmin. You painted his dead wife."

I pretend to squint at the nearest painting. "Really? I can't see it."

She stares at me, then shakes her head. "You don't look

like a New York punk, you know. If that's what you were going for. You look like a cancer patient."

Satisfied with her insult, she turns in a huff and walks back towards Helen, who looks concerned.

I take my time walking around each of the pieces. Even though I painted them, I never had the distance to properly look at them. They're not perfect, but there's a direction here. A future.

I feel people watching me as I circulate, but no one comes up to me. I had prepared myself to see Lachlan, but he doesn't seem to be here. Paddy and Jack are talking conspiratorially in the corner, and avoid my eyes as I walk past.

After completing a lap, I search for Anya. Even though she didn't want me to show these paintings, Anya has been the only person who has supported me the whole way through. My only friend in Rosford. Now that I'm about to leave for good, I want to thank her.

I find Helen frowning in front of one of the larger pieces, and she tells me that Anya is in the office upstairs. I go up and knock on the door.

"Who is it?"

"Me. Can I come in?"

"Ah, the woman of the hour." She's behind her desk, a bottle of scotch in front of her. I wait for her to invite me to sit down, but she just stares. "What have you done to your hair? And what the hell are you wearing?"

"This is me," I say, simply. "You don't approve."

"This is a big mistake. You've messed it all up."

I feel the blow but force myself to keep smiling. "You don't like the paintings."

"How could I like them? She was my friend!" She lowers

her voice to a whisper. "You've painted his dead wife! How is he supposed to react to that? How are any of us?"

"But it's—" I stop myself before I spew any platitudes about the importance of art. How it's the only thing that matters. Truth and beauty — all that bullshit. Anya's right. It's just an excuse.

"You're different than I thought," she continues. "Underneath that quiet exterior, you're a radical. You'll never fit in here. I can't believe I never saw it."

"I don't want to fit in," I say. "I'm leaving."

"What?" There's a look of panic in her eyes. "You can't. You just got here."

"Anya—" I pause. I'm not sure how much to tell her. Anya knew Lachlan before she knew me, after all. But she's my only friend. "Lachlan's a damaged man. He's still grieving for Yasmin. But he's only with me to reenact his relationship with her. The dresses, the hair! Wait till I tell you about that—"

"You can't," she says, matter-of-factly. "He won't let you.

"What do you mean?"

"This isn't Queens, darling. You can't just do things like this without consequences. He'll fight you for every cent. Did you even read your prenup?"

"I don't care." I'd rather go back to waitressing than live with that man. I'm about to explain this to Anya, when Helen interrupts us, her face flushed.

"We did it!"

She pulls me in for a hug. I want to push the two-faced woman away, but grit my teeth and accept it.

"We sold them all!" she says, finally letting me go. "If you agree. Fifty thousand dollars. Not that you need the money, but—" She pauses, as if the words are thick in her mouth. "Congratulations!"

CHAPTER THIRTY

Fifty thousand dollars. That's more than I made during the entirety of last year. More than I *ever* made in a year from a single job.

I extract myself from Helen, then go back downstairs, circling the party one more time to get a last look at the paintings. I won't miss them, these judgmental women of Rosford. And their groping, arrogant men can also go to hell. Aside from Anya, whom would I actually miss? The patronizing doctor? The asshole neighbor? All the other prim women who have stared and gossiped ever since I moved to this town?

Good riddance.

When I get home, I park on the street. I'm soon inside, stuffing my clothes into a bag. Now that the cameras are gone, there's a chance he won't know what I'm doing. I might be able to get away quickly.

Anya's wrong. Given all the shit he's pulled, I should be able to get a real divorce. I might even get enough money to buy a place of my own.

I allow myself to indulge in that fantasy while I pack. No more small towns. An apartment of my own in a small city, with a studio space down the road. Enough free time to work on my next project. An actual television. I'll watch *The Office* the whole way through, volume up. I'll listen to the music I like, without having to feel embarrassed that I'm not listening to Brahms or an opera. If I feel like it, I'll scroll on my phone for hours.

It's my life. No more shame. No more pretending to be someone I'm not.

It takes me ten minutes to finish packing — but then I have another challenge. Homer. I take the carrier from the garage and walk through the house, calling his name softly, then head outside. I'm wasting time, but I can't leave without him. I find the cat at the edge of the property, sitting on a fence post, his eyes shining in the moonlight.

"I know, the night is for hunting. But we have to go," I whisper to him, as I pick him up and push him into the carrier against his will. I stuff some cat treats through the bars, then haul him through the garden to the back door. "I'm sorry, baby. It won't be for long."

I'm in the living room when I hear the sound I dread most.

The garage door is opening.

Lachlan's home.

I leave Homer and rush upstairs to get my bags. I take the stairs two at a time, but I'm not fast enough. When I return, I find him standing in front of the door. His eyes are bloodshot, and he looks like he needs a shave.

"I'm sorry, Lachlan."

He doesn't respond, so I come closer.

"Please move out of the way," I say. "I'm leaving you."
He unfolds his arms, then slowly shakes his head.
"I'm afraid I can't let that happen," he says.
And then he rushes towards me like a bull.

PART 2

CHAPTER THIRTY-ONE

I wake to darkness. Not just the darkness of night time in the suburbs, but complete darkness. I can't even see my own hands in front of my face.

I move my head and it feels like a dozen tiny kittens are scratching at my brain, plucking my neurons with their claws.

What happened? It takes a few minutes to piece it together. I was about to leave, when Lachlan appeared, blocking my way. And when he charged at me, he had something in his hand. Pills. He slammed me to the ground and then twisted my arm until I screamed with pain. Again and again until I swallowed.

I'm lying on something soft, but it's not my bed. It's a mattress. I reach out and feel the ground underneath it. Wood. Am I in the house? He hasn't tied me up and I'm still in the clothes I was wearing.

I sit up with a groan. My head is pounding, and my back and shoulder are sore from where I hit the ground. I feel around with my hands, but there's nothing close to the mattress. I seem to be in the middle of whatever room I'm in.

There's a buzzing sound I recognize. A refrigerator. Has he put me in the kitchen? No — there are floor-to-ceiling windows in the kitchen. Even in the middle of the night, there's light coming in.

I crawl towards the sounds until I can touch the refrigerator, then pull it open.

As light fills the room, I see where I am and what he's done, and my blood runs cold.

I'm in the basement, and it's all back. Nearly everything I gave to the movers is back in its original position. He must have done it while I was at the art gallery.

But how did he do it that quickly? He must have been watching me the whole time through his cameras. He must have intercepted the movers almost immediately after they left the property.

He was ahead of me the whole time.

Aside from the bed and the fridge, there's just one extra item. A small portable toilet in the corner with a wooden lid, on which rest two rolls of toilet paper.

I leave the fridge open and use its dim glow to guide me up the steps to the light switch

I flick it on, then go to the door and try it — but of course, it's locked. I bang on the door a few times, then yell out.

"Lachlan! Lachlan!"

I press my face against the door and continue, screaming until my throat is hoarse. When I can't scream anymore, I pound at the door until my knuckles bleed.

When I stop making any noise, I hear the refrigerator beeping in complaint, so I walk back down. Before I close the door, I see what's inside. There are a dozen ready-to-eat meals, a selection of apples and bananas, and five massive plastic bottles of water.

I close the door, trying not to think about what this means. It's all a mistake. I look around the room, searching for another way out, but the walls are stone, and the ceiling is too high to reach.

It's not a big deal, I tell myself. In a crazed fit, he's locked me in the basement. Once he calms down and comes to his senses, he'll let me go. Or someone will ask about me. Someone will notice.

But then I remember what I said to Anya at the party. I said that I was leaving town. That I was leaving Lachlan. Word will get around. That means no one will come looking.

I feel panic rising in my chest, so I sit down on the steps. The meals, the organization, the heavy door — it tells me that he's had this ready for a long time. He doesn't mean to let me leave any time soon. Maybe ever.

My chest tightens, my stomach tenses. I try to hold off the panic attack by studying the room, looking for a way out. But I know there's no point. He's thought of everything. There will be cameras, too — he'll be watching my every move.

I can scream and pound at the door, and no one will hear me.

I sit with this thought for a moment and let the tsunami overtake me. My heart begins to race; I'm sweating, and the world begins to spin. I lie down on the mattress and wait for the panic attack to end. When it finally does, I begin to cry.

My life is over. As soon as he put me down here, I was dead. He can't ever let me go, because he knows that I'll tell the police — and then *his* life will be over.

I'm dead.

I feel my chest tighten again, and I've soon succumbed to another attack. This one lasts longer, and when I recover I feel desperately hungry. I go to the fridge and take out one of the meals and bottles of water, and force myself to finish both.

As I eat, I decide that he's not going to kill me — if he was, I'd be dead already. But why keep me alive?

There's only one reason I can think of. He knows about the baby. Which means I'm going to be down here for months, if not longer.

My headache dulls and I find my eyes beginning to close. I go to the mattress and before I know what's happening, I'm asleep.

CHAPTER THIRTY-TWO

When I wake, it's dark again. I remember where I am, and feel the familiar wave of panic — but this time, I don't succumb.

I'm not going to die, I tell myself. *He wants me alive.*

My tongue feels scratchy again, so I reach for the water I left beside the mattress before I passed out, but I can't find it. I crawl on my hands and knees to the fridge, and find that there's a new full bottle of water to replace the one I opened before I fell asleep. With the light of the fridge, I look back to the mattress, and see that my food from last night is gone, too.

He was here, while I was sleeping. As I go to turn on the main light, I see that the toilet has been emptied.

I eat, and then do a slow circuit of the room, looking for something I can use to break out. But there's nothing — of course there's nothing. The door is thick metal, the walls concrete.

I go through the boxes in the corner, looking for the photos I found last time, but they've been taken away. There are suitcases of Yasmin's old clothes, expensive dresses packed away without a thought. As I'm crouching down, I feel something in my pocket. I reach in and retrieve the letter I got from the post office.

Her letter.

I sit on the couch by the credenza and rip open the envelope. Two handwritten pages fall out. I skip to the end and see her name.

As I suspected, it's Yasmin's words. My stomach turns as I begin to read.

Alex,

I know I have no right to get in touch, but there's no one else I can talk to. He's got to everyone. They're all on his side. They all believe him over me and I can't trust anyone. I can't even trust my own phone or email. He's tracking everything.

I need your help. Come get me, please. I don't have much time. I'm sitting in the car in the garage. As far as I know that's the only place that he can't watch me.

There are cameras everywhere. He controls everything I do. He chooses my dresses, my jewelry, my hair color. Last year, I told him I was leaving, and he put me in the basement for three months. When I came out, I told one of my friends. She told Lachlan and I was locked away again.

I can't trust them. I can't trust anyone in this town.

It's taken me nearly six months to win back his trust.
I can't risk losing it again.

I have only one chance. Every night he forces me to
take a sleeping pill. I've figured out that he leaves the
house not long after. I have about twenty minutes
before I'm unconscious. I can't drive far, but I've
timed it out and I can get to the first exit off the high-
way. There's a gas station. I'll be waiting in the car
park. I've drawn a map on the other side of this page.

9pm. August 25. Two weeks.

If you're not there, I'm going to keep driving. I can't
stay in this town anymore.

Please be there.

I'm sorry for everything, but I need your help. Please
help me!

Please.

Yasmin.

P.S. I'm pregnant. You're going to have a niece.

As I finish the letter, I feel a rush of shame. This is the
woman I competed with? The woman I was jealous of?

I wonder who Alex is, and why he didn't even open the
letter. It sounds like her brother. I imagine him seeing the
transformation — the hair, the dresses, the personal trainer —

and warning Yasmin away. After she insults him again and again, he gives Yasmin a choice: Your family or Lachlan. She chose Lachlan, and so he cut her off, for good.

I'll never know what really happened. Anyway, he wasn't waiting for her at the gas station. I can imagine her heart sinking as she saw the empty car park. She feels her eyelids getting heavy. The world fades to black.

When she wakes up, she's back in the basement. Eventually, she goes into labor. And when it goes bad, there are no doctors to help her.

She dies. The baby dies.

Two months later, Lachlan sees me in a restaurant. Someone who looks enough like Yasmin. Someone weak and pliable. An idea forms. He can get the love of his life back.

Everything about my life since I met Lachlan has been a replica of her life. The house, the proposal, the honeymoon, the clothes, the hair. Even the sex.

And now this.

It's a tragic story, but as I read the letter again, I feel light. Because even though she failed to escape, he gave her a chance. He didn't want to leave her here forever. He didn't want her to die.

Which means that he'll give me a chance, eventually.

I'll just need a better plan.

CHAPTER THIRTY-THREE

Vomit.

I need to vomit.

I scramble for the toilet, but it's dark and I'm not sure if I'm going in the right direction. Before I can make it, I expel last night's dinner all over the floor. I open the refrigerator and manage to turn on the light, before spending the next half hour bent over the toilet bowl.

Great. Just when I thought it couldn't get any worse. I touch my hand to my stomach, and have the thought that maybe my unborn child is punishing me for what I had planned. If Lachlan hadn't locked me away, I'd be ending the pregnancy right now. But unless someone rescues me soon, that's not going to happen.

I vomit again and again, and when my stomach is finally empty, I look up at the ceiling and scream.

"I hope it dies! Do you know that? I hope I die and that I take it with me. You'll never have my baby! Never!"

The rant continues for another few minutes until I exhaust myself.

I wait for him to come.
He doesn't come.

THE MORNING SICKNESS continues for another week. I scream at the cameras twice more, and then I give up. The room is soundproof. He knows I'm sick because he empties the toilet every night, and he doesn't care.

I try to stay awake at night, but the pregnancy is exhausting me, and I can't seem to keep my eyes open.

I've managed to find the cameras. They're the same tiny black eyes I found inside the house — but these ones aren't hidden nearly as well.

Every day, I read Yasmin's letter, and the connection I feel to her grows deeper. On the eighth day, I search through her desk and find a pile of notebooks. They're filled with sketches — some of birds, others of the meadow behind the house. They're all scenes from outdoors.

She's a great artist. Better than me, at least technically.

In the final notebook, I notice a single letter printed on the corner of the first page. There's another letter on the second, and another on the third. I skip to the middle, and see that there's a small sketch of a woman, drawn with great care. Even though it's tiny, I can tell that Yasmin means it to be a self-portrait.

It's a flip book, the sort of thing I enjoyed when I was a kid. I go through it slowly and spell out the words.

The first 12 pages:

Help me. Help me.

Then:

Kill me. Kill me.

When I get to the sketch of Yasmin, I begin to flip. It shows her connecting a rope to the rafters, standing on a stool, then hanging herself. On the final page, the woman's body is limp and lifeless, her head dropping down, an 'X' over each eye.

I drop the book as if it's radioactive.

———

BY THE TWENTIETH DAY, I feel like I'm actually about to die. My morning sickness has been getting worse each day. Today's session lasts over two hours. I continue retching well after my stomach is empty. I wonder if this is something worse than standard morning sickness. What if the baby's in trouble?

I didn't want this baby. If I were free, I wouldn't be pregnant anymore. But now that it's started to grow, I feel a desperate, elemental need to keep it safe.

And I really, really don't want to miscarry down here. What would he do if it went wrong? Leave me to bleed out on his basement floor?

I can't let that happen. I sit up and look directly at the camera, swallow whatever scrap of pride remains, and begin to plead.

"Lachlan, I need a doctor! I'm worried about the baby. I'm so sick. Please, get me help! I won't do anything, I promise. I'll lie. Just save our baby. Please!"

I give it a minute, then repeat myself.

I do it again and again until I'm too exhausted to continue.

CHAPTER THIRTY-FOUR

When I wake the next morning, Lachlan is sitting in a chair next to my bed.

At first, I feel strangely elated to see another human being after spending so many days in isolation.

"Lachlan. Please—"

He raises his hand to stop me, and so I stop. I'm terrified, and I'll do whatever he asks if it will save my baby.

When he speaks his voice is calm and steady. "I've arranged for the doctor to come and see you. I've told him that you're sleeping down here for peace and quiet. Please don't contradict that story. Please don't tell him any lies about the way you've been treated."

Before I can say anything, he stands up and leaves the room. I wonder if I'll ever be brave enough to fight back. In my head, I imagined that I'd scream at him, curse him, fight him. Tackle him from behind and slam his head into the concrete. Make him bleed.

Could I really do that? I'd never even been in a fight, not even with Damian when he got violent.

No, it's a useless fantasy. I'll never be able to truly hurt him. I'm just a coward. That's why I'm here. I had a dozen good reasons to leave Lachlan before he put me down here, and I never did, because I didn't trust myself.

I expect to wait for another day, but a few minutes later the door opens, and I see Doctor Yang descending the stairs. He's not the doctor I would have chosen — but just because he's a judgmental asshole doesn't mean he doesn't believe in his oath.

He's a real doctor. That means he can help.

Dr. Yang pulls up a chair next to the mattress and asks me questions about my morning sickness. While Lachlan watches, he removes a stethoscope and examines my stomach.

"Is it OK?" I ask.

"There's a heartbeat," he says, turning to Lachlan. "I think we're good."

"What about her?"

Yang frowns at me, then places the stethoscope under my shirt without warning. "Elevated heart rate. She's pale, weak. What are you feeding her?"

"See for yourself," Lachlan says, pointing to the fridge. He glances at this phone, then gives Yang a nod. "I'll leave you to it."

Dr. Yang pulls up a chair next to the mattress. Lachlan gives me a look, before retreating up the stairs. He's trying to warn me — but I don't care. I think of Yasmin's sketch, the limp body hanging from the rafters, and I can't stop myself.

"He's locked me up down here," I say, the words coming out thick and fast. "I tried to leave him, and he put me down here and won't let me go. I haven't seen a soul until today. I don't want to die down here. Please, you have to help me!"

"Hold up," he says. "Slow down. Tell me again. You think you're trapped down here?"

"Yes! For two weeks! I haven't seen a soul until today."

"That's a horrible story," he says, standing up. "Wait here."

"No! Take me with you! He'll kill you!" I don't know if this is true, but I can't just let him leave.

"Please. Leave it with me."

And before I can get up to follow him, he darts up the stairs two at a time and closes the door behind him.

CHAPTER THIRTY-FIVE

Five minutes later, I see that I've made an enormous mistake.

The door opens, and Lachlan comes down the stairs, followed by the doctor.

"I trusted you, Olivia," he says, sitting in the chair next to my mattress. "I told you not to tell the doctor any stories. He's here for your benefit. Your baby's benefit. You had to be selfish, didn't you?"

I glance at the doctor. "Please."

"You thought he would help you? He knows everything."

I can see the uncertainty in the doctor's eyes. "Why are you helping him? You know this isn't right."

"What's right is that we help you carry your baby to full term," he replies, looking away. "That's what's right."

"You don't believe that."

"I believe—" the doctor begins, before Lachlan cuts him off.

"We might as well cut the shit. She's not stupid." He gets out of his chair and crouches beside me. For the first time,

Lachlan looks me in the eyes, and I can see that he's suffering. He doesn't want me to be down here. If I didn't know better, I'd say that he still loves me. Or maybe he just loves what I could be, if I just followed his orders and stopped having a mind of my own. He wants Yasmin. And he can't let it go.

"Several years ago, I helped Yang out of a jam. A gambling issue. Illegal, of course. And since then, I've assisted with investments that have turned him into a rather rich man."

"Blackmail," I say.

Lachlan places his palm on my forehead. "She's burning up." He turns to Yang. "What do we do?"

He stares at me for a moment and I see a flicker of empathy, before the mask returns. "Cut the sleeping pills. They're too strong. She needs natural sleep. And I can give her something to help with the nausea. And because she's not getting any sunlight, we'll need some multivitamins. Vitamin D."

"Sleeping pills?"

"Of course." Yang gives a wooden laugh. "How do you think he replaced your food, the toilet, all of it?"

I turn to Lachlan. "You've been drugging me?"

He taps his foot with impatience. "Anything else?"

"Get a treadmill down here. Or an elliptical. You want a healthy baby, then you'll need a healthy mother. And get her a bucket to wash in. She smells like a vagrant."

"Right," Lachlan says. "We can do that. Anything."

The doctor turns to me. "You crossed the line, young lady. Too many times. And Lachlan isn't quite right. I believe that the world needs more strong men like Lachlan. And I believe that it's time women like you learn to accept the blessings you've been offered. So don't expect the cavalry to come any time soon. I recommend you focus on getting healthy and showing some respect and honor to your husband."

I think they're about to leave when Lachlan suddenly places his hand on my stomach. I see it for sure this time. Love. Uncertainty. It's my chance.

"Lachlan," I say, making my voice as soft as I can. "Why am I here? Just let me go. We can be a family again. I love you. I made a mistake trying to leave."

I think he's listening, but when he turns to face me, I see he's trembling with rage.

"You want to know why you're here? Because you wanted to kill my baby!"

I'm thrown. I had scheduled the abortion in another town. How did he know?

"What—"

"Don't try to deny it, young lady," the doctor says, his voice as stern and patronizing as ever. "I had placed a warning on your medical records, when I heard you were requesting Plan B from the pharmacy. They had to inform me. And I thought Lachlan had a right to know that you were going to murder his child."

"It's not—"

"Enough! I'm not going to debate my child's life with you." He stands up and nods to the doctor. "Let's go. We'll make those changes."

"Wait! What about Homer?"

"He's fine," he says without looking at me. "What do you think I am? I'm not a monster."

Even though there's no hope, I beg for them to stay, to talk, to just be here, to not leave me alone again.

But then the door slams shut, and I'm back with my sick body, my unborn child, and my circling, darkening thoughts.

DESPITE WHAT THE DOCTOR RECOMMENDED, Lachlan drugs me again that night. When I wake the next morning, the room has changed. There's a night light plugged into a socket in the corner of the room and a torch by my bed. There are two large buckets and a towel with various care products.

But the biggest change is the TV and DVD player by the couch. When I go closer, I almost crack a smile. A complete box set of *Friends* and *Suits* sits on top of the pile.

Two of my favorite shows. He doesn't want me to go crazy, after all.

There are other DVDs, mostly boxed sets of sitcoms he knows I like. And at the bottom of the pile is an unmarked case. It looks like the kind you could burn from a computer back when computers had DVD players.

I switch everything on, then carefully unsnap the disc from its case and pop it into the machine. I spend a few minutes figuring out the remote. When I finally hit the right button, an image comes on the screen. The remote falls from my hands and smashes open, spilling its batteries across the floor.

He didn't. He couldn't.

The recording isn't great, but I can tell it takes place in our backyard. There's a fire in the middle of the lawn, piled with a number of rectangular objects.

I go closer to the screen, just to make sure. As if anticipating my needs, the camera moves closer to the flames, slowly zooming in until it's clear what's happening.

My paintings.

All of them.

My paintings weren't purchased by some secret collector who believes in my genius. They were purchased by Lachlan.

And now, they've all gone up in flames.

CHAPTER THIRTY-SIX

Weeks go by. On the advice of Dr. Yang, Lachlan doesn't drug me at night. Instead, he comes down before I go to sleep. He insists that I sit on the floor on the opposite side of the room, facing the wall, while he stocks the fridge, takes away the dishes, and empties my washing water and toilet.

The lights must be connected to his phone somehow. He flicks them on and off three times before coming in, which is my signal to go to the wall. I could try to attack him, of course. I could find a weapon in this room and use it to slit his throat. At night, the fantasies become even more elaborate. I could booby-trap the stairs so he falls and breaks his neck. I could pretend to have a miscarriage, then drive a sharpened chair leg into his heart. I could seduce him into sleeping with me, then rip out his windpipe with my teeth.

So many *coulds*. But then I wake up, and reality sinks in.

First, he has a camera on me. I've no way of knowing when he's watching me. There's no way I'll be able to find and hide a weapon and be sure he won't notice.

Second, there's the fact that I'm three months pregnant. I'm hardly the best candidate to get into a fight.

And third, the most important fact of all: He terrifies me, and I'm a complete and utter coward.

The food becomes progressively healthier. One day, a treadmill arrives. And though I hate myself for doing it, I walk for miles on it every day. I take all the multivitamins he gives me. I try to ration out the episodes of TV, but end up spending most of my time burning through the DVDs he has given me.

One day, I wake to find a dress and heels laid out beside my bed. My instinct is to cut the dress up with scissors. But then I remember Yasmin's letter. He kept her down here until he could trust her.

And how did he know he could trust her? With a series of tests.

Dr. Yang was my first test, and I failed.

This is my second.

After exercising, I clean myself and apply all the products he's given me, even the eyeliner and the perfume. I then put on the dress and heels and spend the rest of the day watching television alone.

I follow this absurd routine for a week. Each day, a new dress appears, with the old one taken away to be cleaned.

Then, a third bucket appears next to the two I use to wash. There's a packet of supermarket hair dye next to it. My hair is still short, barely coming past my ears, but I carefully apply the dye and make myself platinum-blonde again.

When my hair dries, I go to the mirror and study my new appearance. I don't quite look like Yasmin, but I'm getting closer to her again. The only thing that will stop me is my belly, which is already pushing against the tight dresses Lachlan is giving me to wear.

After I've finished, I go to the couch and put on the final season of *Suits*. It's not the same without Mike Ross, but it's comfort food, and while watching, I can almost forget where I am. Sometimes, I find myself talking to the screen like a crazy person, anticipating the lines I know so well.

I'm three episodes deep when the basement door opens. I stand and wait for the light flashes, but they don't come. He's earlier than usual.

"Sit down," Lachlan says.

I follow his instructions and perch on the edge of the couch, attempting to imitate how a lady might sit. He comes over and ejects the *Suits* DVD with a sneer, replacing it with one from a generic case.

My chest grows tight. The last DVD he gave me showed my paintings in flames. What will this one be? How else could he hurt me?

There's only one way.

Homer.

"How the heck—" He smacks the remote control on his knee and presses the function button until the screen changes. "Finally."

I want to turn away, but I know I can't. He wants me to see it, so I have to see it, or he'll find another way to punish me.

Please be alive, I pray, though I'm not sure to what exactly. Jesus? Or what did I say to Lachlan, that time in the chapel? Juju? Karma?

While it loads, he sits next to me on the couch. I wish I knew some kind of martial art. Something with pressure points, where I could quickly dig my hand into his spine and leave him instantly immobilized.

But as the screen loads, I forget about hurting him. Because it's not Homer that I see on the screen, but a ghost.

Yasmin.

CHAPTER THIRTY-SEVEN

It becomes our routine. He visits every night after I finish dinner. It must be late, after he gets home from work, though I have no real sense of time outside of the basement. I wear the dress he provides, heels, makeup, and he sits down next to me on the couch.

And then we watch.

The first DVD is of their wedding day. It's a long recording, but I'm spellbound. It's an exact replica of my wedding to Lachlan. The same dress, the same hair, the same chapel overlooking the water in North Carolina.

Lachlan even says the same vows before kissing her.

The camera then cuts into the hotel room, where Yasmin is dancing in her wedding dress. She does a mock striptease, and then the camera shuts off.

The next night, we watch footage from their honeymoon in Europe. These are short videos shot on their phones, meticulously stitched together.

There are more videos from their life together. Every night, we watch for thirty minutes. If I speak, he immediately turns it off and leaves. The first time this happened, the disappointment was so profound I cried out.

I hate myself for this weakness — for showing him that I want him here, that I need him. I want him dead. I have violent fantasies about killing this man in every way possible. But when he's here, I feel a desperate need to keep him next to me. To touch him, even.

Is it Stockholm Syndrome? Or do humans simply need the presence and touch of other humans?

Either way, I want him there.

So, I learn my first lesson: I stop talking.

IT QUICKLY BECOMES clear to me that these aren't social calls. He's here to teach me. This is my education in all things Yasmin.

We spend a full month watching every recording he has. My dreams — once populated by the cast of *Friends* and *Suits* — start to be filled with *her*. Once we're finished, he looks at me plaintively. "Do you understand what you have to do?"

Of course I do. In a way, I've known ever since I found out about the honeymoon. He wants me to be Yasmin — but not just dress like her or dye my hair to look like her. I have to really *become* her.

"Yes."

We start watching again. When he leaves, I start trying to talk in her voice, which is slightly deeper and more assertive than mine. I try walking like her, too. She's more assured than me and has the grace of a dancer, but I keep practicing.

I practice for another month. Every afternoon, I spend an hour getting ready. I wash, do my makeup, wear perfume — the whole ridiculous process. One day, I see razors beside the bucket, and so I shave my legs and armpits, too. Every two weeks, he makes me re-dye my hair so the roots never show. My belly is growing larger, and new dresses turn up with more room around the middle.

Once we're finished watching the videos a second time, he gives a nod of satisfaction.

I've passed the test.

He holds out his hand and my heart skips. This is it.

"Come with me."

CHAPTER THIRTY-EIGHT

The light is dazzling. It's late afternoon, but the colors are so rich that I feel tears forming in my eyes. The feel of grass under my feet sends a surge of energy through my body.

I'm outside. Not free, not yet. But I'm out of the basement. Two months of work to keep the insane man happy, and I'm out.

I feel something nuzzling around my leg.

"Homer!"

I kneel and let him jump into my lap. Some people say cats are selfish, but it isn't true — they remember the people who love them. I'm relieved to see that he hasn't given him away, or even mistreated him, as far as I can tell.

"Thank you!" I say as Homer climbs onto my legs. "I didn't know..."

"What can I say?" he replies with half a grin. "He's growing on me."

It's eerie how casually he's talking to me. It's like he thinks I'm a kid who's been put in her room for time out. I look towards the back of the garden and see that he's built a high wall at the back of the property so that the meadow beyond is no longer visible.

"Come inside," he says.

My chest tightens. Not inside. Not yet. I'd sleep on the grass if I could.

"Can I see the Sanctuary first?"

"Yes, good idea."

He leads me down the path and opens the door for me. My painting supplies are all there, laid out on the table. There's even an easel in the same place, ready to be used.

I can't believe it. This insane man really does believe we can go back to normal.

No chance.

"Thank you. This is beautiful," I say, putting on my best version of Yasmin's accent. "I'm thirsty. Do you think you could get me some water?"

"Of course, darling," he says. "Wait right here."

And then, to my astonishment, he walks back into the house. I'm alone outside. How is this possible? I don't have a plan of escape. I'd do anything to go back inside — but I can't risk getting put into the basement again. The back fence is too high, as are the fences to the neighbors' houses. And for all I know, the neighbors are his accomplices.

I stand there, ridiculously, like an animal too scared to leave its cage.

But then I hear a sound — the boy next door, in his playhouse — and a plan begins to form.

I walk up to the fence.

"James," I hiss. "James!"

He comes closer to the fence.

"Hello," he declares shyly. "At my school, we have three chickens!"

"James. This is important. I need your mother to call the police. I'm a prisoner. Can you tell her that? Call the police."

To my dismay, he giggles. "Can I have a turn next?"

"What do you mean?"

"He said you would play. But I don't want to be the police. Can I be the prisoner this time? Or can we watch this round first?"

It takes me a second to realize what's happening and see what a mistake I've made.

"What do you mean, watch?"

"Why are you yelling at me?"

I try to calm myself, though I can feel the panic building. He's filming me. Of course he is. He warned this kid before he let me out. It's another test, and I've failed. The walls are already closing in, and I've only been out for ten minutes.

"I'm sorry, James. I didn't know anyone was filming. But it's not a game. He's lying. I'm really trapped."

He's quiet for a moment, and I resist the urge to slam my palm against the fence in frustration.

"He didn't tell you? It must be a surprise." His voice is high-pitched, close to a giggle. But to me, it sounds like the roar of a demon, pulling me back down to hell. "There he is."

When I turn around, Lachlan is marching towards me. His expression is impassive, but when I start to scream, he bends my arm back and slams me to the ground.

"I can hurt this arm so bad that you never paint again," he whispers. "Come quietly."

In the background, I can hear the boy laughing. To him, it's all a game. No matter how loudly I scream, he won't convince anyone that I'm a real prisoner.

So I go quietly back down into the basement.

THE LAST WIFE   197

AN HOUR LATER, the door swings open, and an object is tossed down the stairs.

"Cross me again, and I'll take his head."

The door slams shut. I pick up the object, which is small and furry, and then scream until my voice is hoarse. I know exactly what it is. The tip of Homer's tail.

I sob and sob until I pass out.

Because there is no hope anymore. I'll never be trusted.

I'm never getting out of this basement alive.

CHAPTER THIRTY-NINE

I spend the next morning staring at the ceiling. I wonder if I could loop something through the rafters. Even if he saw me doing it, he'd probably be at work in the city. I'd have hours to go through with it before he found me.

I smile to think of it — the end. But I know that I can't go through with it.

I need to stay alive for the baby.

My bump is noticeable now, not that there's anyone to notice it. Five months. I'm feeling heavy and tired.

Will I really die down here?

It's not even a question, is it? Why would he let me live after I deliver his baby? I'm sure he's already concocted a bullshit story about where I've gone for the people in town. He didn't kill Yasmin, but maybe that's because she was smarter than me. Maybe she didn't blow everything on trusting the good sense of a preschooler.

When I get lunch from the fridge, I see a familiar sight. The buckets for washing have been set up, with a dress and heels. Does he expect me to keep it up?

I've already failed two tests. I told Yang that I was a prisoner, and now I've done the same thing with the boy next door. It seems unlikely he'll trust me ever again.

But I do it, anyway — not for him, but because it's my only anchor in this place, my only real routine. My mind feels like a boat bobbing in the harbor. I'm afraid that if I lose my routines, then I'll slip my mooring and lose control of my thoughts.

When I'm finished getting changed, I go to the television. I have the choice of watching one of my shows again, but instead, I open the DVD of their marriage.

I know it's crazy, but I want to see her again.

I DO this for another month. I never see Lachlan, so he must be either drugging me again or creeping down in the night. The baby starts to kick. I enjoy seeing the skin of my stomach push up. It tells me the creature is healthy — though it also terrifies me, because it makes it real.

I don't want to give birth down here, though I know that's the most likely possibility. One day, my water will break, and Yang will turn up. He'll deliver the baby with no epidurals or pain relief. If there are any complications, they'll save the baby and leave me to die — I'm sure of it.

And if I don't die, will I even get to see my baby? To hold it? To feed it? I can already imagine the separation, the terrible yearning, the torture of knowing that *he* is up there, feeding it, holding it, loving it.

I want to scream.

But instead, I go through my routines. I wash and

change. I shave my legs and dye my hair. I'm holding onto the smallest of straws, the faintest sliver of hope.

CHAPTER FORTY

Every morning, I spend an hour exercising. Then I get ready. I wear her dresses, her jewelry. I do my hair like hers. I watch the DVDs again and mimic her walk.

Finally, I copy her voice in the mirror, like an incantation. I can feel myself inching closer to becoming a perfect copy of Yasmin.

Is he watching me? There are cameras here, though he has a busy job. I can't imagine he watches me from the office, which means most of the time, I'm completely alone, and this routine of mimicry is pointless. Of course, I can't take the risk. I don't know when he might be watching, which means I have to assume he's watching every second.

But I'm not just doing this for him, anymore. I'm doing it for *her*. Aside from Lachlan and Yang, I might be the only person who knows what really happened to her. What her life was really like, at the end.

I remember all my ugly thoughts about her, the intense jealousy I felt when I first moved to Rosford, and I'm ashamed. This is what men do to us: They pit us against each other; they make us compete as if *they* were a worthy prize.

I wish I could talk to her. I want to understand her, beyond the home videos and photos. I want to talk with her about painting, my baby, all of it.

And I want to remember her.

Because if I remember her, then there's a chance that someone will remember me, one day.

THE BABY KEEPS GROWING. Even when I feel like my stomach can't possibly stretch any further, it grows. Whenever it moves, I feel a rush of relief. Without the usual medical scans, I have no way of knowing if it's healthy or not. I fear that every minor pain is a potential miscarriage. I count the kicks, and if a few hours go by without movement, I become frantic with worry.

As I get closer to the birth, I become more obsessive about my rituals. It becomes harder to make myself look like the Yasmin from the DVDs, so I spend even more time in front of the mirror, practicing my accent and mimicking her expressions.

One day, I wake to find that Lachlan has added a dozen more DVDs to the pile. More of my favorite sitcoms. The next day, he comes down and motions for me to join him on the couch. I expect him to play another recording of Yasmin, but to my surprise, he puts in the first season of *The Office*. He sits next to me, unsmiling, as we both watch the show. Neither of us laughs. At the end of the first episode, he gets up and leaves. The television is still playing, and I can see what he's trying to do. He wants to make sure I'm still normal. That I haven't completely lost my mind.

This is another test. After he leaves, I force myself to watch another three episodes. He comes back the next night, apparently satisfied by the results.

I'll get another chance soon. I can feel it.

I'm not going to die down here.

AFTER A FEW MORE WEEKS OF this routine, he comes down with another DVD. This time, he doesn't stay.

I force myself up — a slow process these days — and see that it isn't another sitcom. It's in a generic case, the same brand as the home movies from earlier.

I feel a surge of excitement. Maybe I'll get to see her again. I wonder if this will be scenes from a holiday abroad. Or maybe just clips from the first few months of their marriage.

It loads slowly. For a few minutes, the screen is almost entirely black, the only light coming from a dull white glow in the corner of the screen. I take the remote and skip ahead. After about ten more minutes, the screen suddenly fills with light.

I go closer to the screen, trying to figure out what I'm seeing. Is it — me? A heavily pregnant woman lies on a mattress on the floor. A portable toilet is a few feet away. It's definitely the basement, but there are subtle differences. I can make out the couch and credenza — but no exercise equipment, and no boxes piled along the wall.

The woman sits up, and a few seconds later lets out a bloodcurdling scream. She does this half a dozen times, before lying back down. I go closer to the screen to make out her expression. She's staring at the ceiling. Her lips are moving, but there's no sound.

Then she turns onto her side and starts to weep.

This goes on for another hour, until she goes quiet. She looks surprised, then scared. She rolls off the mattress and looks directly at the camera.

"Lachlan!" she yells. "It's coming! Please!"

She's pointing at the mattress. There's a dark patch where she had been lying.

I suddenly realize what she's saying — and what I'm watching. Her water's broken. She's going into labor.

And soon, she's going to die.

CHAPTER FORTY-ONE

I immediately turn off the TV and sit back on the couch.

It wasn't an accident that Yasmin died — it was a *consequence*. He didn't mean for her to give birth in this basement, but Yasmin kept trying to leave him, to take his baby away. He had no choice but to keep her down here.

And then she died. Their baby died.

This DVD is a warning. But why? I can't go anywhere. I haven't left the basement in months.

It can only mean one thing. He wants to give me another chance.

It's clear from the DVD that this chance will be my last. If I screw this up, I'll die just like Yasmin. And my baby might die, too.

I can't let that happen.

I put the DVD in again from the start, and this time I watch it through to the end.

MY CHANCE COMES SOONER than expected. The next morning, there's a pregnancy dress and a new bottle of hair dye beside my bed, with an extra bucket of water. After an hour of walking on the treadmill, I go through the familiar routine of dying my hair.

Afterwards, I take off my clothes and wash myself. I wonder if he watches me do this. He's barely touched me the entire time I've been down here. It's a relief, of course — but also a problem. If he isn't attracted to me anymore, then it's clear what will happen when I have my baby.

He'll take it away and then kill me.

It sounds so obvious. But then, why is he spending so much time with me? Why force me to dress up and dye my hair? Why does he care about any of that?

He's never hurt me, though. Aside from the two times he forced me down here, he's never been violent.

After I'm finished, I stand naked in front of the mirror and study my strange new form. My hair has grown past my shoulders, almost back to its original length. But what stands out is my enormous stomach. I want to remember the shape of me, the way my stomach extends out like a globe, my enormous new breasts, my glowing skin.

The door swings open. I blink at the burst of light, relishing it before Lachlan shuts it behind him. He looks away while I change into the dress he has laid out. I wonder if he still desires me. Does he find my new body repellant? Or is he already courting another young woman? Is my replacement already waiting in the wings?

Maybe he does want me, but finds it distasteful to have sex with someone against their will. I'm unsure why he draws the line there, but I'm thankful he does. When I'm finished changing, he walks over and places a necklace, earrings, and my wedding ring on the mattress.

"Wear these. We're going out tonight."

"Out?" My voice cracks. It's the first time I've spoken in days.

"We're going to Paula and Jack's house for dinner. It's a Christmas party."

Christmas! I came down here in the summer, and now it's nearly the end of the year.

"We?"

"I can trust you, can't I?"

"Of course!" I say quickly, unable to hide my desperation. "When?"

"I'll give you an hour to get ready."

CHAPTER FORTY-TWO

Has the world always been so beautiful?

We're driving through the surface streets of the town in Lachlan's new Roadster. It's nighttime, and the air is cold outside. The trees have lost their leaves in the months I've been locked away, and the town is spare and gorgeous.

"Now, Olivia. I don't want you to get your hopes up. This is a one-off."

I nod. I had expected nothing less. "I know."

"They're my friends. You remember what happened with the doctor?" I don't respond, so he touches my leg below the hemline. "Olivia."

"Yes."

"They know everything. But they don't want to hear about it, OK? This is a celebration. If you so much as mention what's happened, it's all over."

He made it seem like our marriage would be over — but I knew it would be more than that. For Lachlan, the end of our marriage means the end of my life. It's all the same to him.

"What do I say, then? About where I've been?"

"With your mom in Iowa. It's been a difficult pregnancy." He turns a corner, and I'm aware that we're close. I wish we would stay in this car forever, watching the beautiful world pass by. "Figure something out."

"I can do that."

"It's not a choice. You won't see your baby. Ever. Not if you cross me."

He makes it seem like all his friends know about the basement, but that can't possibly be true. One or two of them, sure, but not all. Rosford is a town of snobs, but they can't all be psychopaths. Dr. Yang kept his mouth shut because he owed Lachlan a colossal amount of money. But Paula and Jack? Helen and Paddy? Why would they go along with it?

At the same time, I couldn't risk it. I need to be smart this time. I'll only get one shot.

"I know," I squeak. "I promise."

"Good girl," he says, squeezing my leg. His hand lingers on my thigh, and it takes everything in my power not to shudder with disgust.

PAULA AND JACK'S house is much bigger than Lachlan's. It's a long, bizarre structure with garish fake columns and an absurd number of dormers scattered across the roof. It must have been stylish at one point, but it's been bastardized over the years by renovations and extensions.

If I needed more proof that Paula doesn't have a tasteful bone in her body, then this house is it. I walk slowly down the path to the front door. I'd be happy to stay outside in the cold night air, but all too soon I'm standing inside their doorway, taking off my coat.

"Olivia! You're as big as a house!" Jack pulls me in to kiss my cheek and holds me for a second too long. His hand rests firmly on the small of my back until I move away. I can tell what he's doing. It's more than a quick grope. He's planting the seeds for a future rendezvous. Is this what happens in Rosford after a few years? Couples grow bored and sleep with each other? "You're more beautiful than ever," he whispers in my ear.

I send a frightened glance to Lachlan, who is already deep in conversation with Paula. I'll be damned if Jack is the one who gets me sent back to the basement.

I go through to the living room and pretend to study the paintings on the walls when Helen comes over.

"They're prints. I told her which ones to buy."

I smile, wracking my brain for something to say. It's been so long since I've had to sustain a conversation.

"Where's Paddy?"

"Paddy's at Paddy's house. With the girls."

I obviously can't keep the look of surprise from my face. *Paddy's house* — that means they're separated. A more socially adept person would know what to say, but I can't think of anything.

"He's a bastard if that's what you're thinking. They all are, except for your Lachlan, of course. He's such a thoughtful guy. You've really landed someone special."

The smile on my face is so fake that she must be able to see the truth.

"Yes," I say eventually.

"Alright then," Helen says, raising her eyebrows and walking off. I go back to the paintings until Paula announces that it's time to go to the table to eat. I'm relieved to see that I'm placed next to Lachlan and Helen. That means I won't have to spend the night fending off Jack's hands under the table.

After a few comments about my pregnancy and Iowa, the conversation predictably turns to real estate.

"How's the building going?" Jack asks Lachlan.

"What building?" Helen asks.

"Our Lachlan has acquired a building in Queens. He's going to become a slumlord."

"It's hardly a slum," Lachlan says. "Middle-class accommodation. Families."

"Sure, sure."

"Where in Queens?" Helen asks.

Lachlan shrugs, and Jack laughs. "He's being shy. It's on Bryant Street. Gorgeous building, though massively inflated valuation if you ask me. Lachlan here must know something about the market that the rest of us don't."

Bryant Street. Surely not?

"You didn't?" I ask.

Lachlan looks down at his food and doesn't respond.

Helen makes a show of looking from me to Lachlan. "Didn't what? Olivia, what's going on?"

"I used to live on Bryant Street," I say quietly.

"That explains it!" Jack declares. "I didn't think you'd be that stupid with your money. It's a grand romantic gesture. Not sure you'll be staying in Queens when you go to the city, though. And you didn't even tell her!" He covers his mouth with his hand. "Wait, did I spoil the surprise?"

"It's not like that," he mutters. "It's just an investment."

I know I shouldn't say anything in front of the others, but I can't help myself. After six months in the basement, I no longer know how to keep my thoughts to myself. "Where is he?"

"He?" Jack declares. "The plot thickens."

Lachlan looks at me for a moment, and I wonder if I've made a big mistake. Six months ago, I would have known to hold my tongue. He wipes his mouth with his cloth, then looks around the table.

"I guess I might as well tell the whole story. If it's OK with you?"

I feel their eyes on me, and I give a small nod.

"Before I met Olivia, she was in an abusive relationship. I helped her get out — that's how we met, actually. But it always annoyed me that this guy was just living a normal life after what he did to my wife. So—"

"You kicked his ass!" yells Jack. I can see he's already filled his glass three times during dinner.

"No," Paula says, whacking Jack with her napkin like he's an overzealous puppy. "Lachlan isn't a violent man."

"You're not saying this asshole is paying you rent?" Jack asks.

"Let me finish," Lachlan says. "I raised the rent, then evicted him. Then, I made sure it was known among the major landlords in the city that he was a horrible tenant. His credit score should be affected. Any luck, and he'll have a hard time getting another place in the city."

I look at Lachlan in astonishment while Helen and Paula burst into applause. "Our hero!"

"You did that?" I say quietly. "While—"

He cuts me off before I can say something stupid. "While you were away at your mom's. Yes. I had to." He leans across and kisses me on the lips. It's the first time he's kissed me since locking me up, and it makes me want to vomit. "I love you."

I move my lips as if whispering it back while Paula lets loose a wolf whistle. "You guys are too cute."

"I'm still disappointed you didn't kick his ass, but well done! Who says romance is dead?" Jack grabs Lachlan's shoulder and gives him a rough shake, then moves to fill his glass. "We need another bottle to toast our hero!"

"I'll get it," Helen says, rolling her eyes.

As soon as she's gone, I see my chance.

"Where's the ladies', Paula?" I ask.

I pretend to follow her instructions, then double back and follow the corridor into the kitchen. I find Helen looking into an enormous pantry full of wine.

"I don't need help, Jack." She glances back, then flashes a smile. "Sorry. I thought you were someone else. I was afraid he was going to try to cop a handful." She pulls out a bottle, reads the label, and puts it back. "Ever since Paddy and I separated, he's been trying it on. I'm going to have to change numbers. Honestly, the number of times that man has sent me pictures of his penis. I should print them out for the next gallery show."

She says it like a joke, but I find myself unable to smile.

"Don't worry. I can handle myself. Ask me the definition of a functioning alcoholic, and I'll point you to Jack." She looks at another bottle. "And ask me the definition of playing dumb, and I'll point you to Paula. Honestly, she'd put up with Jack murdering the neighbors if it meant she got to keep this hideous house."

Again, I don't know how to reply. She glances back at me. "Christ, listen to me. Maybe I've had one too many."

"No. Sorry. I didn't know any of this."

"You keep to yourself. That's wise. Not sure how healthy it is, but I admire it. Mostly, anyway."

"Hey," I blurt out. "Can I borrow your phone?"

"Excuse me?" She straightens, frowning slightly.

"Sorry. I got rid of my phone after the exhibition. Too much social media." I'm talking fast and everything I say sounds completely unnatural. "I need to text something to my mom or she'll call Lachlan."

Helen looks like she's about to object, but then changes her mind and reaches for her phone.

"Lachlan didn't just get you a new one?" she says as she unlocks it. "Didn't know he was so frugal."

She goes back to comparing the wines. I open the messaging app and search through her contacts list until I see Anya's number. Out of all the people I've met in Rosford, she's the only one that Lachlan doesn't seem to like or get along with. From what I can tell, she hates Lachlan.

It's still a risk — but it's all I've got.

I quickly scrawl a text.

> Anya, this is Olivia Gibson. I'm being held captive in Lachlan's basement. Help me, please. There are cameras. I've been there for months. Lachlan's a liar. Don't believe him. Please help me! DO NOT RESPOND TO THIS NUMBER.

I make sure the text has been sent, then swipe to remove it. I had considered just calling the police, but I didn't know how to get any privacy with Helen's phone. Besides, there was always a chance the cops were in Lachlan's pocket or that he'd be able to talk his way out of it.

"Olivia, are you OK?" Helen asks as she locks her phone.

She says this with such intensity that I feel like crying. I know that I can't trust her — most likely, this is a test Lachlan has set up, just like with the boy next door. But even false sympathy from another human is too much for me. I look away before she can see the tears forming.

"I'm fine. It's just the pregnancy. Messing with my hormones."

"It was the same with my girls. I burst into tears at the supermarket when I forgot my purse. Eight months in. The cashier almost let me go without paying." She touches my hand. "Well, I'm here if you need to tell me anything."

Jack calls for wine, which breaks the spell. I remember who this person is — who they all are. I think of Yasmin and mimic her broad smile.

"Don't worry about me. My life is perfect."

CHAPTER FORTY-THREE

Lachlan is pleased with my performance. On the drive home, he reaches across and touches my hand. It takes all my energy not to pull away in disgust.

"What happened to Paddy?" I ask to distract him.

I can tell immediately that I've said the wrong thing. He pulls his hand away and squeezes the steering wheel.

"Helen asked him to leave," he says eventually.

The follow-up escapes my lips before I can stop myself. "But why?"

When he replies, he speaks slowly, as if trying to restrain his anger. "There is no why. There is right and wrong. He made a mistake with a girl at his firm." *Girl.* Men like Paddy break the female gender into two broad categories: girls and wives. Everyone else — children, older women, anyone not considered to be sexually viable — didn't even register.

"He cheated on her," I say.

"She broke up her family. There's no excuse for that." It takes me a second to realize I've misunderstood what Lachlan is telling me. The 'right and wrong' doesn't refer to the affair but to Helen's decision to kick him out. "She should be strong."

"Like Paula." Not for the first time, I wish I had Yasmin's counsel. I'm running my mouth with a man who controls my freedom.

He doesn't speak for most of the ride home. When we turn onto our street, he slows down and glances at me. "I know you think I sound regressive. Paddy and Jack are assholes. I get that. But Paula and Helen made their choice a long time ago. For better and worse. And let me tell you, there's been a lot of 'better' for both of them. Helen has children, and the consequences of her poor choices and intolerance land on them. They only get to see their father on the weekends, and who knows how long that will last? Paddy will probably marry the girl from the office and move to another town. It's a tragedy. And a completely avoidable one if Helen just sucked it up and realized that life isn't always going to be a fairy tale."

A thousand responses are floating through my mind, but for the first time on that car ride I decide to keep my mouth shut. After he parks, he touches my hand again. I'm worried that he'll want to take me to bed, but after a moment, he frowns.

"Let's go quietly," he says. "We don't want to wake the neighbors."

THE NEXT MORNING, I find a newspaper beside my bed. The Sunday edition. It's enormous but a pleasant surprise. I spend the next two hours poring through the news. There are elections in the city. In my old life, I would pride myself on staying informed about local events. My ex Damian, for all his flaws, was active in grassroots politics. He knew every issue backward and would furiously debate anyone who dared express an opinion that didn't precisely match up with his own.

I say 'for all his flaws', though I suppose for most people, this *is* a flaw. But I found his stubborn passion massively attractive when we first met. He was the kind of person I had never found in Iowa. Someone who was unapologetic about his passion for art and politics and books and — for a time, at least — *me*.

For many years, I tried to keep up with his knowledge of local politics, even though he never treated me like his equal. Reading the newspaper now, though, in this basement, my stomach as large as a minor asteroid, the news might as well be coming from an alien species. I read stories about schools and sports, real estate, and relationships. The opening night of a mediocre play. New films. New books. Wars overseas. Trade. Quarterly earnings. Strong opinions about all the above.

Crime, too. I read about theft, corruption, and fraud. Stories about murder.

And that's when I find it. The reason Lachlan gave me this newspaper. It's not because he's sentimental or kind. He wants to tell me something.

The story is sandwiched between a column on drunk drivers and photos depicting a spate of smash-and-grab robberies.

Damian Holland. Murdered at night in Queens in a robbery gone wrong. His body was found down an alleyway. Five bullets. Four to the chest and one to the head. No witnesses, no clues. *A talented artist and beloved member of the community,* the journalist writes. *His family begs for witnesses to come forward.*

I glance up at the ceiling to the cameras. This might be a warning, a signal of what he can do when pressed. But I don't think so.

He did this for me. He murdered my abuser. This is a twisted act of love.

The maniac wants me to thank him, as if this is what I wanted. But all it does is tell me exactly what this man is capable of — and what exactly he's going to do with me, if I fail another one of his tests.

It's only a matter of time.

Anya, I think. *Where the hell are you?*

FOR THE NEXT WEEK, I wait. It's not like before. Time passes slowly, painfully. The routines aren't enough to fill the time, and I can't focus on the television.

Because now, I have hope.

My back aches from the mattress, and it takes a full minute to stand up in the morning. Instead of the intense cardio I was doing at the beginning of my pregnancy, I spend my exercise time walking slowly.

Every night, I count the kicks. They're aggressive, energetic. Despite spending my pregnancy in this prison, the baby feels healthy. The supplements and the strict diet must be doing the trick.

But as the days pass, I know a deadline is approaching. Anya needs to come now, or I'm going to have this baby down here. And then, anything could happen — including a repeat of what happened to Yasmin.

My baby and I could both die down here.

She has my message, so what is she waiting for? I wonder if she confronted him, and he convinced her that the message was a lie or a joke. Or maybe he hurt her. Maybe he saw the walls closing in and decided to kill her. That might happen in a movie — but I can't see Lachlan doing that. He's too smooth. He'd find another way to put her off.

Then it happens. I'm lying on the mattress, trying to sleep, when the door swings open. Anya stands in the darkness. Behind her, I can see snow.

"Merry Christmas," she says. "Let's get you the hell out of here."

PART 3

CHAPTER FORTY-FOUR

She tosses me a jacket and helps me up the stairs. When I'm out in the yard, I look back at the house. Despite everything, it's still beautiful. But I suppose only a child would think beauty and evil couldn't go together. I sometimes wonder if the opposite is true. Maybe they *always* go together.

"You want to take a picture?" Anya says. "Let's go. We don't have much time."

"I want to burn it to the ground," I say.

"Well, that'll have to be another day, my pregnant pyromaniac. Lachlan's watching all of this."

That's enough to make me follow her around the side of the house, through the gate to the street. The snow is light, though I'm unsteady on the icy sidewalk. I lean against Anya as she shuffles to her ancient BMW.

"It's icy tonight. I'll put the chains on later."

"Chains?"

"I told you," she says as she helps me into the passenger seat. "We're getting the hell out of here. No more Rosford. Somewhere Lachlan won't find us."

I wait till she's started driving before asking where exactly we're going.

"There's a cabin in the Adirondacks," she says, referring to the mountain range in the north of the state.

"Anya?"

"Yeah?"

I point to my stomach. "I can't be stuck in a cabin in the snow. What if my water breaks?"

"It's the Adirondacks, honey, not the Himalayas. You'll be fine. There's a hospital thirty minutes away. Honestly, it's probably closer to a major hospital than here. The most important thing is that he doesn't find you."

I can see the pattern of snow falling in the streetlights.

It's OK, I tell myself. *I can trust Anya.*

As we reach the end of town and pull onto the freeway, I close my eyes and let myself feel it. I'm free. Never again will I be locked up like an animal. Never again will I be treated like a slave. Never again will someone take control of my body.

Free.

I can feel my eyes water, and before I know it, I'm sobbing. Anya touches my shoulder, and I feel myself breaking down. Everything I've been holding in for the last six months just to keep myself alive. It all comes out.

When I finally stop crying, I don't feel at peace. I don't feel happy or content.

I feel angry.

"I want to go to the cops," I say.

"We need to get you safe first."

"No, the cops."

"I don't know how to explain this..." Anya sighs. "But we can't trust the cops."

I'd had the same thought, but I protest anyway. "That's bullshit. This isn't some third-world country."

"You don't understand. It's a small community, and Lachlan has lived here for a long time. People respect him. He gives to charity. If there's a dispute in his marriage—"

"Dispute!" I feel my voice begin to break. "I've been a prisoner for six months!"

Anya is quiet for a moment. "I'm so sorry, darling. He's a bad man. He's clearly dangerous. But you have to understand we can't trust anyone in Rosford. Let's just get away, then we can go to the cops in another town tomorrow."

"Tomorrow?"

"I promise. Before we do, though, I'm going to ask you to do something difficult."

"What?"

"In case you have trouble in court or with the cops." She takes from her pocket a small digital recorder. She presses a button and then hands it to me. "Speak into this. And tell me everything."

BY THE TIME I finish my story, we're deep in the Adirondacks. Anya had made it seem like we'd be staying close to a major town, but as the hours went by, it was clear that we wouldn't be anywhere near a hospital.

The snow cover gets deeper. At one point, we stop for Anya to put the chains on. I get out of the car despite the cold. I want to spend as much time as possible outside. Anywhere without walls.

When we get on the road again, I ask Anya why it took so long to get me.

"I'm grateful," I say quickly. "But I was worried you didn't get my text."

"I'm sorry. I had to make a plan. I knew Lachlan would be watching everything from the cameras on the property. That's why I chose Christmas. He's out of town for a few days."

"Where?" I pause, and then keep talking. "Wait, who cleaned out the toilet then?"

"He's only just gone. To London, I think."

"His sister? But the baby's almost due. What if I go into labor?"

"I don't know, Olivia! That's just what he told me. He's got cameras on you, doesn't he? Maybe he'd get that doctor to help you and take the next flight." She smiles. "Can you imagine how much he's losing his shit right now?"

I try to feel happy at the thought of Lachlan panicking, but all I feel is a rush of anxiety. Crossing my arms, I try to remember what Lachlan said about his sister, but I can't remember any details.

"I'm sorry you couldn't see your family at Christmas," I say.

"It's OK. You got me out of a trip to Minnesota in winter. I should be thanking you."

"Is that where your family is from?"

"Yeah. Parents are still there. And my brother. We're a lot alike, you know. We both came from the Midwest to New York to dive into the art world. And we both got chewed up and spat out." She gives me a tired smile. "You know, every single person I met in New York who made any progress in that world had a trust fund. Every single one. What does that say?"

I'm about to respond, but she keeps talking.

"It turns out you need money to live an artistic life. Money drives it all. And so what do we do, Olivia and I? We marry rich. You don't need to say anything. I know you told yourself you loved Lachlan, just like I said I loved my husband. But would I have taken the same leap if he didn't have money? Because I always knew what it meant, just like you did. It meant freedom to do what we loved. To actually live how we wanted to live."

She bites her bottom lip and shakes her head like she's trying to dislodge something from her brain.

"But then, it turns out that the men we marry are pricks. First, they drag you to the suburbs, then leave you there while they spend most of their lives in the city at work. They get you pregnant so they can have a family they never see. And finally, when you cross the Rubicon and lose whatever sexual capital you once had, they cheat. By that point, you're stuck."

She slams her fist onto the horn of the car again and again. I'm worried she's going to crash, but she soon regains her composure. From what I knew from Lachlan, Anya's husband had left her a decade earlier with a son and massive legal bills from the divorce. I'm guessing that those years had been extremely difficult.

She's acting strange — unsettled, fidgeting, emotional. Shouldn't she be trying to keep me calm?

Maybe it's just the holidays. Christmas has a way of making people feel lonely.

"I didn't know you wanted to be an artist."

"I told you, darling. I'm just like you."

"Do you still paint?"

"I wanted to make movies, believe it or not. Art films." She snorts. "What a joke. Anyway, as soon as I had Simon, that dream was gone. I tried to let it go and put all my attention on my boy. It never leaves you, of course. That's why I always understood why you didn't want to keep your baby."

"How did you know that? Not even Lachlan was supposed to know."

"Rosford is a small incestuous town," she says as if this explains how my most intimate medical decision became common knowledge. "People talk."

I look outside. We haven't passed another car in nearly an hour. I touch my stomach and am suddenly aware how much trust I'm placing in this eccentric woman. She saved my life, and has helped me ever since I moved to Rosford — but then why do I feel so uneasy?

"What people?"

"It's such a beautiful place," she says, ignoring my question. "But I hate it. I feel like I've been slowly suffocating ever since I moved there. I suppose I'll wake up one day and be as brain-dead as Paula."

The snow picks up as we drive into the hills. If I wasn't running for my life, I'd suggest getting off the road as soon as possible.

"Did I tell you why I left home?" I ask.

"Wide-eyed girl with creative dreams. I told you, we're the same."

"It wasn't just that. My mom — she was abusive. Like, mentally abusive, I guess. She would scream at me for no reason. All the time."

"Ah, that's horrible," Anya says, though I can tell she isn't interested.

"I'd hear her talking to herself," I continue. "And one day, when I was sixteen, she came home from her job as a receptionist, and she was bleeding. She'd cut herself right there in the office. Apparently, she'd been acting weird for months. They tried to keep her on..." I stare out the window. The only person I'd told this to was Damian. He used it against me in arguments for years after. Called me crazy, just like my mother. "They put her in an institution. So, I emancipated myself. Got a job after school to pay rent. As soon as I graduated, I got the hell out of there."

"But now?"

"She's fine. Acts like a normal midwestern woman. But she's on serious medication. Will be for the rest of her life."

Anya brakes suddenly as a deer crosses the road. "Stupid animals. I swear they have a death wish."

"Hey, can I ask you a question? Why did you stay in Rosford, then? If you hate it so much?"

"Because of my son," she says, suppressing a yawn. "The schools are amazing. And the connections... I didn't want to take that away from him."

I understood. After all, what were her options if she wanted the best for her son? The kids from Rosford go on to Ivy League schools. They become lawyers and doctors, bankers and politicians. If she moved somewhere else, she'd make that future much less likely for her son.

"For our kids, we make difficult decisions about how we live," she says. "We make certain compromises."

What compromises? The phrase is loaded — but I don't have the energy to learn more about Anya's life. I think of Lachlan again, and my chest tightens. I concentrate on my breathing to ward off an attack.

I just need to get to the police. Then I'll be free.

BY THE TIME we arrive at the cabin, it's after midnight. By my calculation, we're at least two hours from any kind of town, though I'm too tired to bring it up. She's lied to me — but maybe that's just to get me here.

There's no way Lachlan will be able to follow us. Tomorrow, I'll convince Anya to take me to the police — and if she doesn't agree, I'll use her phone to dial 911. Either way, tomorrow will be the last day I live in fear of Lachlan Gibson.

Anya parks in front of a garage attached to the cabin. It's a replica of an old log cabin but is clearly a new build. With the engine off, all I can hear is trees moving in the wind. The snow falls silently around us.

Anya places her hand on my back and shines her torch on the steps to help me up.

"I hope you understand," she says after knocking on the door. "This wasn't easy for me."

"What are you talking about?" I say. "Why are you knocking?"

I want to keep asking questions — but I hear floorboards creaking inside, and I already know the answer — the impossible answer. It's too late.

The door opens, and I see his face.

Lachlan.

"Darling, you're here at last. Come in out of the cold."

CHAPTER FORTY-FIVE

Before I know what's happening, I've launched myself onto Anya.

She topples into the snow under my newly immense weight and I'm on her, screaming curses, hitting and scratching her face with my janky nails. I've never felt so angry in my life. I want to kill her — but I only have a few seconds to land my blows before Lachlan is pulling me away. Gripping my upper arms, he drags me inside the cabin and pushes me onto a double bed. I try to scramble back up, but with my weight I'm too slow.

He locks the door behind him. And that's that.

I'm a prisoner again.

And this time, I know I'll never be free again.

I DON'T CRY. I keep waiting for the tears to fall, but they don't.

I'm just empty.

There's nothing left.

They're going to take my baby, then kill me.

Who will ever find me, up here? They'll get away with it, too. Who will suspect Anya and Lachlan of my death? There won't even be a body. They'll just dispose of me somewhere, bury me in the woods, and I'll never be found.

Finally, there's no hope. All these months of kidding myself. Of making plans, following orders, as if my time in the basement was just a temporary sojourn, and not the final destination.

My life ended when he locked me in that place. It ended, maybe, when we met that first time in the restaurant. Since then, the clock of my life has been running out.

I look down at my stomach.

The days I have until I give birth will be the last days of my life.

AT SOME POINT during the night, the door opens and someone slides a tray of food along the floor. I don't want to eat, but then my baby kicks, and I know this isn't about me anymore. If I don't eat, the only person who will suffer is my unborn child.

I bring the tray up to the bed, and see that they've given me two TV dinners — one steak, one fish. Once I start eating, I can't stop, and I demolish them both.

Afterwards, I lie on the bed and wait for morning.

WHEN I WAKE, I have a raging headache. Anya is sitting on a chair in the corner of the room, looking at the snow falling outside.

As I remember what she did, I try to launch at her — but something is holding me back. My hands are each cuffed to metal chains attached to loops drilled into the walls.

"I'm sorry it had to be like this, darling," she says. She almost sounds bored.

I curse her out. She winces at first, but remains mostly impassive. There's a long scratch across her cheek from my fingernail last night. I'm pleased to have done even that much damage, but I wish it would have been worse. I continue screaming at her for a full minute.

"Are you done?" she says, as I take a breath.

"You're worse than him."

"How do you think?"

"He's deranged. You're not."

"I need the money," she replies. I can almost see her shrug, as if to dismiss the accusation as naive. "He made me an offer. A very lucrative offer. It pays for everything. My mortgage. My son's education. All my debts. Even my retirement. I was in a hole after my husband left me. I was a few months away from losing everything. My boy would be at public school, and I'd be scrubbing toilets."

"When?"

"What do you mean, darling?"

"When did it start?"

She looks confused, then bursts out laughing. "Oh, for years. We had the same deal with poor Yasmin."

It takes me a second to understand what she's saying. My entire relationship with Anya, from that first meeting in the Sanctuary, was fake. Everything she did was on the instruction of Lachlan. And everything I told her was reported back to him. That's why she told me not to exhibit those paintings. And that's how he knew I was going to leave him.

"You killed Yasmin, too."

"No," she says softly. "That was the last thing he wanted."

"She wouldn't have died if you took her to a hospital."

The accusation lands, but she just gives an exhausted sigh, like the world-weary European she pretends to be. "That wasn't an option. She made poor decisions, and had to live with the consequences. Though haven't we all, Olivia?"

I want to continue with my accusations, but I realize it's pointless.

"Is he going to kill me?" I say.

She just stares at me, sadly, and I see the truth. Either he'll kill me, or she will.

She's been waiting for me to die this entire time — with every mistake I've made, she's been expecting Lachlan to give up on me and finish me off. But now that I'm here, nearly ready to give birth, she sees exactly how it will go wrong.

Even if he wants to keep me alive, she'll find a way to finish me off.

For her son, she'll tell herself. *Because she has no choice.*

I turn away from her and shut my eyes, and I don't open them again until I hear the door close.

CHAPTER FORTY-SIX

At night, I wake to the sound of an argument. It's dark and they're in my room, their voices just louder than a whisper. My brain feels heavy from whatever drugs they're giving me, but I force myself to stay awake.

"It's in the cloud," she says. "If I die, it goes straight to the police."

"You're bluffing," he replies. "How much have I given you already?"

"Not enough. Not for this."

He gives a moan of anguish. What's in the cloud? It sounds like she's blackmailing him. "Don't you see why I have to do this?"

"I see that you're batshit crazy. But I don't care. My hands are dirty. I see that. But once this is all over, I need to be set up for life."

"I don't have it."

"You're lying."

"No." His voice gets louder. I can feel that he's standing

close to me. "You'll come back for more. This will never end."

"For me it will. I want to forget this ever happened. I'll delete the file. No one will ever know."

The file. I suddenly know what she's using to blackmail him. The recording she made of my story. I told her everything. She said it was for the police, the courts — but all she wanted was leverage against Lachlan.

He's silent. I feel his weight on the edge of the bed. Then, his hand on my stomach. He keeps it there for a moment. "Fine."

I hear her breathe a sigh of relief. She slaps my foot under the comforter. "We both know this isn't going to end in happy families. What are you going to do to her?"

"I'm not going to do anything to her," he says, raising his voice. "This is my wife."

"Oh my God! She's not your wife anymore. I hope you're not thinking of keeping her?" She's talking about me like I'm a stray cat that's come inside for a saucer of milk. I can't make out what he says in response, but it's enough to make Anya storm out of the room and slam the door.

I almost admire her courage. She knows what Lachlan is capable of, but still she blackmails him. At any moment, he could end her life. But she has that ruthless bravery that allows her to stare him down, and win.

This is what we are, I suppose. All of us. Even me. Beneath the tame politeness of our suburban selves is a tiger, sharpening its claws, waiting to pounce.

I SPEND the next week praying for my water to break. I'm in bed most of the time, groggy from the drugs they're giving me. One night, a storm rages; another, it snows heavily, silently. I wouldn't be surprised if we're trapped up here.

From my window, I see nothing but forested mountains. A carpet of white pine. I know there must be other cabins in the area, but I've no idea how close they are or how to get to them. I could smash the window and run, but even if I wasn't caught immediately, I'd freeze to death.

It's a stupid fantasy. My stomach is enormous and I can barely walk. I just have to get this over with. Give birth to a healthy child. That's the only purpose I have left. Once it's over, maybe I can find hope again.

Or maybe they'll just kill me. And maybe that will be better than my other fate — to go back to the basement for the rest of my life.

SOMETIMES AT NIGHT he comes in and touches my stomach. Each time, I feel a rush of anger, but I remain perfectly still. I don't want him to notice me. After everything that's happened, I'm still terrified of this man. I hate him, but I fear him.

I'm still a coward. Desperation, it turns out, doesn't cure cowardice. I already know I'm going to walk to my own death, rather than risk a real fight. One night, he comes in with another man. From their whispered conversation, I understand that it's Yang. He touches me. Takes my blood pressure. Listens to my breathing.

I feel an injection in my arm and I'm asleep again.

WHEN I WAKE, the first thing I notice is the pounding in my head. My tongue is thick and I'm dehydrated. There's a drip in the corner of the room, but at some point they must have decided to disconnect it.

The second thing I notice is my stomach.

It's smaller, saggier, like a punctured tire.

I let out a scream of anguish. They've taken my child — I didn't even get to feel it leaving my body. They just knocked me out and took my baby like thieves in the night.

I scream again. I'll kill them — I mean it, this time. They've gone too far. I try to get up, but my legs feel like jelly. Whatever they injected me with has left my body limp and weak. They haven't even bothered chaining me to the wall.

"My baby," I say, quietly.

I let the words sit in the air.

"You've taken my child!" The words come out fast, unfiltered. I'm soon screaming. "My baby! Give me my baby! Give me my baby!"

Suddenly, the door flings open. I turn to see Lachlan standing at the stairs.

"What are you doing?" He quickly closes the door behind him. I can see that he has a bundle of blankets in his arm.

I realize that I'm crying. I quickly wipe away the tears.

The baby begins to stir in his arms, and he bobs them up and down. His motions are frantic and I desperately want to tear my baby away.

"You're gone." There's a flash of fear in his eyes.

I try to stand up and move towards my baby, but only

end up falling in a heap on the floor. I see now that he's brought the baby to breastfeed.

"You're gone," he repeats, and takes a step back.

"No!" I scream from the floor. "Lachlan! Please, I'll do anything."

"I'm sorry," he says.

The baby is crying now, and I join in, a primal chorus that can only be silenced when my child lies in my arms. "I'll do anything."

But he just looks at me like I'm a crazed animal, a threat that needs to be contained.

"I can't trust you with her."

I keep crawling towards the door, but in a heartbeat it closes behind him, and I'm alone.

HE THOUGHT I was insane then, but in the days that follow, my mind truly slips its mooring. My thoughts loop wildly, uncontained by logic or reason. Hours pass that I can't remember. I scream and pass out and scream some more. I see no one and hear no one.

As the days pass, I tell myself I want to die, though there is still a candle flickering inside me — for her. The only reason to stay alive.

My baby.

Sometimes it works, and I regain my mind again. But mostly it doesn't. He brought her down to me. I could almost touch her. And then he left.

He comes in to give me food without her, and I scream at him. I've been chained again, and I pull at my bindings, desperate to be free so I can tear him apart like a banshee.

He puts my food on the table next to my bed and leaves without saying a word.

I have nothing left. No energy to stop the wild thoughts. They toss me around like an old sailboat in the open sea. They become ten-foot waves. I'm hopeless against them.

I'm drowning.

CHAPTER FORTY-SEVEN

On the third night after the birth, I wake to the sound of screaming. It's high-pitched, rhythmic, like a ritual incantation, and it immediately silences the swirling, despairing thoughts.

My baby. I have to get to her, to soothe her. He doesn't know what to do. I try to sit up, but my arms are still chained to the walls. I pull again, and again. I can hear him walking her up and down the halls, coming right up to my door and then walking back. He's doing this on purpose, because he knows what she wants.

After a few minutes, I hear Anya's voice. When Lachlan speaks, he sounds desperate, angry. He doesn't want to give his baby to Anya, but she's the only one who can give him a break.

The crying moves further away, and then a door shuts, and I can't hear her anymore. But I can feel it. She's still calling for me. She needs me.

I have to get to her.

The next morning, I hear their voices in the hallway. I

strain to hear the sounds of the baby, but it's just Anya and Lachlan, talking intently.

"I have to go. If my son spends too much time with his father, he starts listening to Joe Rogan and watching the UFC. God help me, I'm not letting that man undo 17 years of hard work."

"Stay longer. With what I'm paying you—"

"You're paying me to keep my mouth shut, not to be a goddamn wet nurse. You have the mother right here."

"I can't trust her."

"If you can't trust her—" Anya pauses, and I fill in the gap.

If you can't trust her, get rid of her.

"I'm not doing that."

"Then let her feed the baby. She's like this because you took the baby away."

"You didn't hear her. She's lost her mind!"

"And why do you think that is, after what you did to her?" Another pause. "What we did to her. Fine. Anyway, the baby needs the colostrum in her breast milk. She's going to be feeding eight times every day. Maybe more. You want to do all that?"

He mutters something, and Anya laughs.

"This whole circus is because you wanted to resurrect Yasmin. To get back the life you lost. So give her the baby. If you don't soon, she won't be able to breastfeed at all."

"No," he says. "She's too far gone."

"You can't have it both ways." I hear footsteps grow louder, then a knock at the door. "Goodbye, Olivia. I'm going now."

I feel like the whole performance has been for me, her attempt at kindness. Does she expect me to thank her, or give a friendly goodbye? As I picture her standing outside my door, all I can think of is winding the chains on my hands around her thin neck and strangling the life out of her.

"Call me with an update," she says to Lachlan, with a labored sigh. "Let me know what you decide."

Decide. Over the next day, that word sticks in my mind. Lachlan has a decision to make. Does he let me be a mother to my baby, or does he kill me? It wouldn't be hard to finish me off and bury my body somewhere in the mountains.

But I have a decision to make, too. Anya's conversation made one thing clear. He wants me to look after the baby, and the only reason he doesn't is because he thinks I've lost my mind.

She's right — of course she's right. Lachlan didn't just want a baby. He wants a family. That's been his goal all along.

Though I hate to give Anya any credit, she's given me hope that I might see my daughter again. And that hope is all I need to settle my mind. I don't need to be free. I don't need to have my own life. I just need to be with my baby.

I TELL myself that he needs me. He'll soon get sick of the wakeups, the diaper changes, the feeds. They can't live without me.

The fantasy runs deep. The separation is worse than anything I've ever felt. I just want to hold her again. I'd give anything — I'd do anything. I'd never speak a word of the last six months again in my life, I'd play happy families for the rest of my life, if only I got to be with her.

My daughter.

Next time the door opens and Lachlan comes in, I'm calm. I still want to kill him, and I'm aware that my eyes are twitching, but I keep myself from screaming out or lunging at him.

"How is she?"

He stares at me, apparently confused by the question. It's like a wild animal learning to speak, I suppose.

"Healthy," he says, then he leaves.

It's a start.

When he gives me breakfast the next morning, he looks like a wreck. His eyes are bloodshot, his face pale, his face unshaven. For the first time since we met, he doesn't look in complete control. He's been defeated by the most powerful force in the universe — an unhappy infant.

"Tough night?"

He flashes me an angry look, as if I'm mocking him. That's exactly what I want to do, of course, but I keep my expression fixed.

"Not settling," he mutters. "It's like she's in pain."

"It's probably just gas. Do you know how to burp her?"

"Of course—" he begins, then shakes his head. "Honestly, you could fill an encyclopedia with what I don't know."

"I can help."

He just nods.

We have the same exchange when he brings in lunch; and then at dinner time, Lachlan comes into the room, his index finger to his lips. He's holding a blanket. He walks slowly towards me, then lowers it into my lap.

"She's a girl."

I look down at the tiny wrinkled creature. She has a patch of brown hair, a small mole on her arm, a diaper that seems far too big for her body. She's small, perfect, alive. I place my little finger in her hand and feel an overwhelming need to keep holding onto this creature, to protect her, to love her.

"Her name is Lydia."

His voice is like a sledgehammer.

"Please," I say, though I'm not even sure what I'm asking. "Please."

"You won't do anything stupid, will you?" he asks. "You must do everything I say, darling. For her."

I feel the urge to rip his eyes from his skull. Reach down his throat and pull out his entrails, like a character from a video game.

But that's just a fantasy. I'd never be able to do it. And even if I could, I can't take the risk. I don't trust him.

I force the words out painfully. "I'll do whatever you want."

CHAPTER FORTY-EIGHT

I'm woken in the middle of the night by her screams. They're louder this time, and as I open my eyes I see that she's in my room.

"What's going on?" I croak.

He lays her beside me on the bed and unlocks my chains.

"Please," he says. "Help her."

While he stands over me, I remove my shirt and let the infant sit against my bare skin. While she lies near my nipple, I massage my breast, trying not to panic. Is it too late? She doesn't seem to know exactly how it works, but her mouth moves around me. Miraculously, after a few minutes, she latches. It takes some time, but I eventually feel the milk flow.

"You can go to bed," I whisper, without looking up.

As soon as he leaves, I begin to cry. I honestly didn't think I'd ever get to see her again, but now here she is. My baby. My daughter. My entire life.

I keep her pressed against my breast, patting her whenever she starts to doze off. When she finally finishes, I place her next to me on the bed. Even though she can barely move yet, I surround her with a wall of pillows. For the next three hours, I watch her sleep, counting her breaths, looking for any sign that she's unhappy.

She wakes crying, which I soon discover is from a soiled diaper. I clean her with tissues I find on the table, and then let her lie naked on the bed. I talk to her the entire time, telling her about myself, about her family, about where she comes from.

She feeds again, and then falls asleep.

BY THE TIME Lachlan comes back, the sun has been up for hours, and I'm starving. I'm about to feed her again and my breast is out. I resist the urge to immediately cover my body in front of this man. It's been over eight months since we've had sex, but the possibility has been there ever since he locked me away.

And who knows? Maybe this maternal scene turns him on more than all the thick makeup and tight dresses I used to wear for him.

But I don't cover myself. Soon enough, Lydia latches and begins to drink. Lachlan sits on the edge of the bed — softly, respectfully — and watches. He sniffs, and when I take my eyes off Lydia I see that he's crying.

Is he thinking of Yasmin? She came so close to doing this before she died. Does he blame himself? Is this an attempt to atone for what he did to her? To resurrect not only her, but their baby?

When Lydia finishes, he lifts her up. It feels like he's slicing off my limb, but I let him do it. I wait for him to hand-cuff me to the bed, but this time he just shuts the door and locks it behind him.

I get out of bed and go to the window. It's locked and triple-glazed, but that's not even the main deterrent to escaping. There's a thirty-foot drop down to the forest floor, and I'd be sure to break a leg or impale myself on something hidden by the snow.

But even if I could make it down alive, I wouldn't leave without Lydia. I'm never leaving her again.

I stretch out my legs. I'm still sore, and I won't be running any time soon, but I'm relieved to find I can move like a human again. My body is healing.

I walk up to the mirror to see my new shape. Though my stomach is greatly reduced, I look like a mess. My roots are coming in, and my skin is blotchy. I wonder how long it will take for Lachlan to give me a bottle of hair dye and a new outfit. I won't fit any of Yasmin's old dresses for a while, but maybe he'll want to put me on a new regimen.

I'd do it, too. For Lydia.

Will it work? Every time he's trusted me, I've betrayed him. He must know that I'd do it again. He still believes that we can be a family. Can I ever convince him that I want a normal life? The thought of him touching me makes me want to vomit. I'd have to let him hug me, kiss me, sleep with me. I'd have to fake orgasms in bed and fake pleasant conver-sation at dinner parties. I'd have to fake my entire life — every little detail, forever.

I'd try, for Lydia. But I know it won't last. I'd slip up, and eventually, he'd come to see that I had to die.

I need to escape from here, in the mountains, while he thinks I'm weak.

Because if I go back to that basement, it's only a matter of time before he kills me.

CHAPTER FORTY-NINE

We soon slip into a routine of sorts. He brings her in once during the night, then again in the morning while he exercises. He doesn't even bother locking the door. I can hear him playing classical music on the other side of the house.

I try to imagine him swinging kettlebells to Bach, but the scene is too absurd to picture. That's always been part of the allure of Lachlan, I realize. He's rich, handsome, and fit, and never seems to break a sweat. He gives the illusion of another kind of life, one that doesn't require you to bang your head against the wall, day after day, just to survive.

I let three days pass with this routine, mapping in my head my plan of escape. It seems too simple to actually work, but it's all I have. With every day that passes, I'm closer to returning to the basement, where I have no chance of escape whatsoever.

On the fourth day, I decide to take my chances. I feed Lydia to sleep, and as soon as I'm sure she's down, I wrap her in blankets and try the door. Just as I thought. He hasn't bothered to lock it. I tiptoe out into the hallway. The floorboard creaks, but the music is so loud that I'm not worried. I go down the small corridor to the front door. His jacket is hanging on the hook, and I take it and wrap it around my shoulders.

Now all I need are his keys. I can't see them near the door, and I'm about to attempt to explore the rest of the house, when I feel a rattle in his jacket pocket.

There they are. The keys to the Roadster.

It can't be this easy, can it? It's been a long time since he's left the house, and he's been sleep-deprived for over a week. Maybe he's just getting sloppy.

I unlock the front door and step out onto the porch. The snow is thick on the ground, but the day is clear and calm. The sun is low against the horizon.

"Let's go, darling," I whisper to Lydia as I descend the steps. "We're free."

I'm soon standing next to his Roadster. There's a fob with a button to unlock it, but that will give off a loud beep that's sure to alert him. I pull at the fob for a second until the plastic gives way, revealing a key inside.

Perfect. I quietly unlock the car, then go around to the passenger side, where Lachlan has already installed a car seat for Lydia. I place her in gently, and manage to get her clipped without waking her up. Then I jog around to the driver's side and get in.

The car is low to the ground, closer to a go-kart than a regular car, and there are buttons everywhere. For a second, I panic. I haven't driven a car since Rosford, and that was an SUV in the suburbs. In Queens, I didn't even own a car. And the Roadster isn't a car for regular people — it's for enthusiasts, people who love the roar of engines, people who have opinions about brands of tires.

Lydia makes a noise and twitches her arm. It won't be long before she wakes.

Screw it. What choice do I have?

I take a second to figure out where the handbrake is, before turning on the engine. It lets out a roar — much louder than I had expected — and when I reverse out of the park to face down the hill, I feel the tires slipping on the snow.

That should have been my warning to give up, but by then it was too late. As I tap the gas, the car lurches down the hill. I see Lachlan in my rearview mirror, standing outside in the snow. The roar of the engine must have cut through his classical music. For some reason, he doesn't look angry. No. He's calling something out.

In fact, he looks scared.

You should be scared, I think. *Because it's over now, and you're going to spend the rest of your life in jail.*

It's only as I take the first corner down the hill that I realize how wrong I am. He's not scared for himself — he's scared for his daughter. Because the road is covered in a layer of snow and ice, and the car is lacking the one feature I need to get down the mountain alive.

Snow chains.

That's why he didn't bother locking the door. He knew I literally had no chance of escaping.

I manage to keep the car from drifting off the road on that first corner, but as I pump the brakes, I feel it twisting behind me. I can see another corner up ahead — and beyond it, a steep bank.

There's an even chance I'll spin over the edge. Lydia is in the front, which means she doesn't have the protection of a normal car seat. I can't risk it — even if it means my life is over. Even if it means I never see her again.

I'm picking up speed and quickly losing control. Just before I hit the corner, I swing the steering wheel as hard as I can and hit the gas once more, forcing the car to crash into the side of the hill. Snow is dislodged from the bank and slams onto the hood of the car. Lydia begins to scream, and in the rearview mirror I see Lachlan running awkwardly towards us along the icy road.

I look down the mountain. I could run, but he'd catch me — unless I left Lydia behind. If he decided to stay and look after her, then I might be able to get a head start. I might even be able to get to another cabin, or even just find another car. Then, I could call the police. By the end of the day, he might be in prison, and I'd be with Lydia, forever.

But that's a fantasy. After the birth, I can still barely walk, let alone run for miles in the snow. How far would I really get? It wouldn't be hard for Lachlan to put chains on the tires and drive after me.

Besides, I'm not leaving her ever again.

As Lachlan gets closer, I unclip Lydia from her seat.

"I love you," I whisper.

And then Lachlan opens the door and rips her from my arms.

CHAPTER FIFTY

"That was very stupid," he says, grabbing my wrist and forcing it into the cuffs attached to the wall. I can hear Lydia crying in the back room. She's been crying ever since Lachlan forced her from my arms.

"Why do you always betray me? Every time I give you an ounce of freedom, you try to destroy me. To destroy *us*. Everything we could have together. Think of Lydia! You could have been a mother. We could have been a family. But no. I can't trust you."

He cuffs the other hand so tight I feel the metal cutting into my skin.

"I just wanted us to be a family. Why is that so hard to understand? I did everything for Yasmin, too. I gave her the house of her dreams, money, beautiful clothes, all of it. And just like you, she couldn't compromise for our family. I loved her. I loved our child. Just like I love you, Olivia! I'm trying to give you everything you could ever want, and all you do is push me away."

Lydia's screams grow more intense, so he raises his voice.

"I give you everything, and you spit in my face! You don't even try! We could have been happy. Imagine it. Lydia playing dolls in our backyard, while you paint, and I—"

He breaks off and wipes the tears forming in his eyes, then looks behind him. He suddenly seems aware of Lydia's screams, and without another word, he leaves the room.

As the key turns in the lock, I try not to think about what he said. Not just the words, but the tense.

You could have been a mother.

We could have been happy.

It's the tense of someone who's given up on me.

If I'm lucky, I'll go back to the basement. But I wouldn't be surprised if he kills me and tosses my body off the nearest cliff.

Either way, it's over.

I hear another door slam, and the house is silent again. I feel like I'm waiting at the foot of the scaffold, about to be led to the hooded executioner waiting with his sharpened axe.

I've read that people who are waiting for death remember their childhoods, their parents, their siblings. But all I can think about is Lydia. What will happen to her? Will he control her like he tried to control me? Will he force her to dress and talk and act the way he chooses? Will he find another mother for her?

I try to imagine her walking to school, riding a bike, going to prom, getting her first job, leaving for college — all those milestones of a normal, happy life. But I can't picture any of it. Not with Lachlan as her father.

All I feel for my daughter is dread.

"I'm sorry," I whisper, as tears begin to fall. "I failed you."

WHEN HE OPENS MY DOOR, it's daytime. I haven't slept. He's showered and clean-shaven, and aside from the dark circles under his eyes, he looks normal again.

"Time to go."

I stare at him, unable to form a sentence. I'm guessing my attempted escape has changed his plans. I've become too much of a risk. He can't leave me with Lydia here while he sleeps, which means he never gets a break.

What's he going to do back in Rosford, though? Drop her off in the basement at night and tell everyone in town that I'd run away? I could live with that, but it's hard to see how people in the neighborhood wouldn't ask questions. People might have thought I was strange — even crazy after the exhibition — but would they really accept that I'd abandoned my newborn child?

Or maybe he's going to tell everyone that I'd died in childbirth? But how long would that lie keep before someone found out the truth and came looking for me?

He unlocks the chains around my wrists and watches me as I stand up. I reach for the water on the nightstand and finish it in one go. As soon as I'm finished, he grabs my wrists and tapes them together behind my back. I try to pull away, but I'm weaker than ever.

He puts his hand on my upper arm and pulls me to the living room.

"Look at you."

Anya is sitting in an armchair in the corner of the room. She's in a black dress and black stockings — the uniform of the art world.

"What are you doing here?" I ask.

"What did you think? Lachlan's going to stuff you into his trunk like a prisoner?" The thought hadn't actually crossed my mind, though now that Anya mentioned it, it seemed more likely than not. "You need a chaperone back into town."

I turn to Lachlan, who pushes me onto the couch. "Stay here while I get Lydia ready."

I wriggle awkwardly until I'm sitting upright. "Where is he taking me?"

She stares at me without answering.

"You don't need to do this, you know," I whisper. "We could go to the police. I could testify—"

"Stop." She takes a deep, exhausted breath. "You know the difference between children and adults?"

"Anya, please."

"Indulge me. Children think the world is full of possibilities. They think that decisions don't have any consequences. That mistakes can be undone. When a child thinks about their future life, there isn't just a fork in the road, but an infinite number of different paths to take." She laughs. "It's not true, of course. But that's what they believe. When you become an adult, you realize that some decisions can't be undone. Some paths can't be walked back. And as you go even deeper into your life, you realize that there isn't even a fork in the road anymore. There's just the road. Single-lane. No options. No choices. Just one set of necessary outcomes."

"Fate," I whisper.

"No, not fate, you simple child! *Consequences.* I was desperate and I agreed to help a man with his marriage. Here I am. You were desperate and convinced yourself to fall in love with a sociopath. Here you are. These are choices." She waves her hand like a magician finishing her trick. "That's life."

"I don't believe that's true."

"I know you don't, darling. That's why you're still a child." Footsteps in the hall. She stands up. "But it doesn't matter what you believe. It won't change anything."

Lachlan enters the room holding the inner capsule of the car seat, a diaper bag over one shoulder. Lydia is already strapped in and asleep.

"Let's go."

He heads to the door, and Anya points for me to follow. We're soon standing on the porch watching Lachlan fit the capsule into the car. It's snowing again.

"Maybe you're right," I say. I feel a glimmer of hope in the way Anya is arguing her case. She wouldn't talk to me like that unless she was unsure of herself. If I can just keep her talking, then maybe I have a chance of convincing her to do the right thing. "We don't have a thousand choices. But there's still more than one. You don't have to do this. I'm going to die down there. And someone's going to come looking for me. I have a family back home. Friends. You'll never get away with it."

The Roadster's engine revs angrily as the car reverses out of its park. The chains Lachlan has installed leave tracks on the fresh snow. He toots his horn, then disappears around the corner.

"Let's say I concede the point. Maybe there are choices," Anya says from behind me. "But the fact remains, darling. They're not yours to make."

I turn to face her, wanting to argue my case, just in time to see a shovel come flying at my head.

CHAPTER FIFTY-ONE

"Honk!"

I open my eyes and try to cry out in pain, but there's something blocking my mouth. I'm lying on my side on a thin carpet, my knees tucked into my chest. My wrists are still taped together painfully behind my back. My lips have also been sealed shut with tape. There's an engine rumbling underneath me, but we're not moving.

I'm in the trunk.

The crazy bitch put me in the trunk of her car.

"Honk!"

I can make out the rumble of other engines. Headlights. I must be on the highway.

We start moving and my head bounces against the floor. I want to scream out again, but panic will only make things worse. If I don't breathe steadily through my nose, I could suffocate.

I stare at the door, looking for ways to escape. A popped trunk on the freeway — that's all it would take. Someone would see me, gagged and bound, and call the police. But the

back of the door is smooth, and we're traveling so fast I can't
be sure I wouldn't roll out into traffic.

I feel us turn and slow down. We must be taking an exit
off the freeway. But where? Rosford? Lachlan expected her
to follow him back home, but why would Anya do what he
said? She's made it perfectly clear she wants him to kill me.
Maybe she's decided to do it herself. We could be going deep
into the woods in Vermont or Maine for all I know.

I picture her opening the trunk, letting me run a few feet,
before shooting me in the back.

The ground will be frozen. Has she thought about that?
It will be almost impossible to dig a grave in this weather. It
won't stop her, though. She knows Lachlan can't be trusted
to keep me hidden.

One day, he'll make a mistake, and Anya's life will be
over.

She has no choice but to kill me.

As we slow down, I hear another horn, fainter this time,
followed by the sound of cars driving slowly past. We're not
on the freeway, but we're not in the middle of nowhere,
either.

We stop and start a few more times, before dropping
suddenly down a steep hill. I find myself rolling painfully
against the back of the trunk, my head slamming back again
as the ground levels out.

The car moves extremely slowly for a few seconds,
before doing a sharp turn and coming to a stop. The engine
goes off, and there are no other sounds around us. No cars,
no people. Not even the sound of Anya from the front of
the car.

I don't know where we are — but I do know one thing.
We're not at Lachlan's house. She's disobeyed his instruc-

tions. I run through the possibilities in my mind, and not one of them leads to a happy ending. I feel my chest grow tight. My breathing is picking up, but I can't get enough oxygen with the tape blocking my mouth. As my heart races it occurs to me that it could all end here, in the trunk of this car.

I kick out with my legs, again and again, trying to force my foot through the metal. I hear movement from the front of the car, followed by a door opening and slamming shut.

I kick again. She's not going to leave me here. This isn't how I die.

It works. The trunk pops open. She stands there staring at me for a moment while I scream at her through the tape. Behind her, I can see a low concrete ceiling and bright LED lights. A parking garage.

"Jesus, Olivia. Did you really need to kick the car like that? This is a rental." She rubs the car like it's a child with a sore knee. "It's nice, isn't it? My SUV doesn't have a trunk like this. And I had to get you out of the cabin somehow."

I keep making noises until she raises her finger to her lips.

"Now, before I let you out, I have a few rules. No running away. No trying to attack me. Remember, I can call Lachlan to throw you in that basement at any point. OK?" When I don't respond, she reaches in and pinches my arm. "OK? Otherwise I'll be forced to hurt you."

She raised her right hand, and I see that she's carrying a small gun. I do my best attempt at a nod, and she snorts like this is the punchline to a joke.

"Come on then." She grabs my legs and swings them over the edge of the trunk, then pulls me up by my arm. "Watch your head."

As soon as my legs touch the ground, they buckle under

me. I fall towards Anya, who catches me and pushes me back against the car.

"Take a minute. Let the blood come back."

I look around me. I was right. We're in an underground car park. It's small, though. About thirty spaces at best, and it's completely empty.

"You're wondering where we are?" she says, tracking my shifting eyes. "I could give you three guesses, but we're on the clock. We're at the site of your triumph. The Rosford Art Gallery."

She must notice the wrinkle in my forehead, because she shakes her head. "All in good time. I have a surprise for you. You might also be wondering why I had to put you in the trunk. The answer is that there's a hundred cameras on the road between the cabin and Rosford. No offense, but it's not a good idea for me to be seen with you right now."

Before I can react, she gives me a push. I stumble away from the car, but manage to regain my balance. She slams the trunk shut and clicks the beeper to lock the doors. "Come on."

I'm led to a door in the far corner of the car park. I glance at the roof, and spot the familiar half-sphere of a security camera. If she's so worried about being filmed, then why did we come here? The art gallery must have security cameras everywhere.

But as we push through the door to the elevator, I have a thought. Anya is the executive director of the gallery. Maybe she was able to turn off the security for a night. But why are we even here? She can't kill me in these offices. She'll never get away with it — it's literally the place that implicates her the most. And it's no place to hide a body, either. During the day, the area is full of people.

The elevator dings and we step inside. I'm still thinking through the possibilities when she presses the button for the top floor.

The top floor. I suddenly realize what she's planning.

She's going to throw me off the roof.

CHAPTER FIFTY-TWO

I try to force myself through the elevator door just as it closes, but it's too late. I turn to Anya, trying to plead through the tape on my mouth, but she just watches me with mild curiosity, like I'm an animal in a zoo.

I want to launch myself at her, but my hands are taped together and I'm still weak. So instead, I throw my body against the wall of the elevator and do my best to press the button for every floor.

"Juvenile," she says, sounding annoyed. The bell for the first floor dings, and she moves between me and the door, raising her gun. "Don't be stupid, now. That's not going to work."

Of course it isn't. Nothing will work — but this is my life. I'll try anything just to slow down the journey from here to the roof.

As the second-floor door opens, I feel my vision cloud over. I lean back and breathe in slowly until it clears.

The third floor opens and I feel a surge of energy.

There's light. A light!

I want to scream, but I can still barely make a sound, so I push forward into Anya as hard as I can. It doesn't work. Anya plants her feet and pushes me back, as if I'm no stronger than a child — which I guess is true these days. I slam into the side of the elevator and fall to my knees. I try to scream, but my voice is still muffled by the tape.

When the elevator dings for the top floor, she kneels beside me and rips the tape off.

"No!" I sob. "No, no, no."

"Come on." She seems impatient, almost bored, as she cuts the tape on my hands. "This has been a long time coming."

"No, please."

Anya pulls me up. I try to resist, but she's too strong for me, and I'm soon stumbling onto the roof of the art gallery.

"We once put a sculpture garden up here," Anya muses, as if she were taking me on a tour. "But we had to shut it down. Some health and safety person said it was too danger- ous. There's only a three-foot fence around the edge of the roof, you know. It does seem like a design flaw. But architects are like artists, you know. They care more about beauty than the lives of other people."

She gives me another hard push between my shoulder blades.

"Why are you doing this?" I ask, my voice shaking wildly. I'm still hyperventilating and can barely get a sentence out. "Why here? They'll find the body, you know."

"That's the point." She shoves me again. "It's an easy sell. Postpartum depression. You're a mess. Everyone already thinks you lost your mind when you cut off all your hair at the exhibition. That's what we told people, you know. That you had a mental breakdown and went back to live with your mother. Then you came back here and threw yourself off the edge. There's a symmetry to it. A beauty, even. It's an aesthetic act. You'll join the ranks of other famous suicides." She gives a sniff. "Well, you would, if Lachlan hadn't destroyed all your paintings. He pretends to be such an aesthete, but these finance people are all meatheads underneath all the money."

"No, please, no!" There must be a way to reason my way out of this. "They'll see the marks on my wrists."

"Self-harm. Or maybe sex games?"

"The basement—"

"Don't kid yourself. They'll never get that close. Who has the motive? According to the GPS on my car and phone, I'm currently in Boston on a college visit with my son. And Lachlan's at home with his baby, wondering where his unstable wife has gone. Who else would want to kill you?"

I search my mind for more reasons why her plan won't work, but I can see that she'll have an answer for all of them. I *was* acting a little crazy before Lachlan locked me in the basement, and I never made any real friends in Rosford. No one would be completely surprised if I killed myself.

"You were my friend," I say, pathetically, as she pushes me closer to the edge.

"Don't take it personally. I'm a great actor."

I drop to my knees and scream as loud as I can. Anya stands over me. I can see the same bored smile. I look for some sign of uncertainty, some evidence that she might not go through with it.

But there's just that same, slightly indifferent expression.

She kicks me with the tip of her black boots, and I yell out in pain.

"Get up."

I look over my shoulder. I'm only six feet from the edge of the roof. "No. I won't."

"Yes, you will." She kneels beside me and places her gun under my jaw, pushing gently. "I can still make this look like a suicide. I'll tell the police you stole my gun. It won't be hard."

"No!"

She gets up and walks behind me. There's a moment of silence, and I wonder if she's thinking about her plan — but suddenly my neck snaps backwards. I feel excruciating pain. She's got a handful of my hair and is pulling me to the edge of the building.

I scream again. But soon it's not going to matter. We're at the wall now. She pulls on my hair once more, so hard that I'm forced to stand.

I can't help but look down at the concrete courtyard. We're so high that when I hit the ground my body will split open like a ripe mango.

This is the end. I'll never see my baby again, and there's nothing I can do.

Maybe Anya is right. Maybe there's one path in life. One inescapable line of dominoes.

I'm waiting for that final push, but there's a sound that makes Anya pause.

The soft ding of the elevator.

Anya instinctively looks over her shoulder — and that's all I need. I charge into her with what little energy I have left, my shoulder slamming into her side so that she stumbles into the fence. I keep charging, and it's enough for her to lose her balance.

For a second, I'm watching her fall over the edge, her mouth wide open.

I try to twist my body away, but the momentum is too strong, and I'm falling, too.

Head-first, I'm following Anya to my death.

CHAPTER FIFTY-THREE

The back of my head slams into concrete and I feel blood rush to my head. I can hear Anya screaming — how is she still screaming?

I quickly realize that I haven't fallen beyond the fence. I'm hanging upside down from the side of the building. Still alive. Someone's hands are locked around my right thigh, their body weight stopping me from falling to my death.

And as they pull on my leg, I realize that it isn't Anya that's screaming. It's me.

I take a breath.

I'm not dead. But I'm not safe yet, either.

"You're too heavy," the person yells out. It's a woman's voice. "I'm not strong enough."

"Please!" I sob. I make the mistake of looking down, and my body jolts with panic. She's down there. Anya. Not a person anymore, just a dark shape on the concrete below. A body. A corpse. Flesh and organs and blood.

A melon, smashed.

"Stay calm!" the person yells. "I need your help. Lift

your hands behind you. You can reach the edge of the wall. Use that to take a little of the weight."

I do what she says, but I'm too weak to lift my body.

"I can't!"

"Just try! I'll do the rest!"

I place my hands on the corner of the wall and try to follow her instructions. She pulls as hard as she can, and I come up a little, but then fall back to the original position.

"One more time!" she yells. "Give it everything! On my count."

On three, I pull again — and this time I feel her pull even harder. I finally come tumbling over the fence, slamming into the ground on my shoulder, before rolling onto my back.

I open my eyes and look up at the night sky.

I'm alive.

Anya is dead — but I'm alive.

"Helen!" I exclaim, sitting up and seeing that she was my savior. "You saved my life. Thank you—"

I trail off. Because I'm not free yet. Not by a long shot.

Because Helen has retrieved Anya's gun. And she's pointing it right at me.

"WHAT THE HELL WAS THAT?" she asks. I expect her to be triumphant after saving my life, but there's panic in her eyes. She's breathing heavily. I note that her hand is unsteady. It would only take a twitch of her finger to end my life. "She's dead."

Shit. All she saw was me, pushing Anya to her death. She says it almost like a question — then repeats it, more forcefully.

"She's dead. Anya's dead."

"Helen, please—"

"I need to call the cops."

No! Not the cops. As soon as they find out Anya's dead, they'll contact Lachlan, and he'll run. With all the money he has, I'm sure he can afford to quickly disappear.

Disappear with my baby.

He probably already has a plan, just in case.

"Helen—"

"Shut up!" The gun shakes wildly. She's almost hysterical. "I always knew you were crazy. I took your side, you know. Paula wanted nothing to do with you. But I saw you had talent, even if you were eccentric. But this!" She sobs, then wipes her eyes with the hand holding the gun. It takes her a second to realize what she's doing. She points it back at my chest, then pats her sides. "Damn. Where's my phone?"

"She was trying to kill me," I blurt out. "You saved my life."

"I should have let you fall. That was my—" She paused, searching for the right word, before giving up. "You killed her."

"She was trying to kill me, Helen. I can prove it." When she doesn't yell at me, I keep going. I have an idea — half-baked, but maybe enough to convince her that I'm not a killer. "Remember when I borrowed your phone at the dinner party? A few months ago? Check the archived messages in your messaging app."

"I have to call the police."

"Do this first. Please! He has my baby!"

She looks down at my stomach, and a small frown creeps onto her face. "You had your baby?"

"It's a girl. Lydia."

"Where is she? Who has her?" She glances down at her phone and taps at the screen. Three taps. 9 1 1.

"She's with Lachlan."

"The father. What's the problem?"

"Helen, please. Read the text."

She looks down at the phone, then lets out an exhausted sigh. I see her swipe away and tap a few times. "I don't know how to use these damn things."

"Archived messages."

"I heard you the first time," she snaps. It takes her a few goes. She glances up at me every few seconds to make sure I'm not about to charge her.

Then she sees it. And her face goes white.

"What is this?"

"The truth."

"He locked you up?"

"In his basement. For my entire pregnancy."

"What about Anya?"

"She helped him. I thought she was helping me, but she was working with him. The whole time."

"And she brought you here to kill you?"

With every word she says, the story sounds less and less plausible. "She didn't trust Lachlan anymore. She wanted to make my death look like a suicide."

She shakes her head slow, then fast. "Why would he do this? It doesn't make any sense."

"I don't know, Helen! Maybe he wanted the perfect family, and when I wouldn't give it to him, he snapped. Or maybe he's just a sociopath!" My voice is becoming more frantic. If Helen calls the cops, Lachlan will find out Anya's dead, and he'll run. I might never see Lydia again. "Lower the gun, please! I have to get my daughter back."

"But why would Anya help him?"

"Money!" I'm crying now. "I don't know, OK? I've been locked away for six months, they tried to kill me, and all I want is my baby!"

She stares at me, then lowers her gun.

"It never made sense that you'd disappear for that long, especially after the exhibition. And I always wondered where Anya got the money to live here. The alimony is drying up now her son is almost eighteen. And she's been acting strangely ever since you moved here. I thought you were just her pet project." She pauses. "We have to call the police."

"Helen!" I protest. "It'll be too late. They won't believe me. Someone will give him a warning and he'll run—"

"Let me finish," she says, holding up a hand. "We'll call the police *after* we get your baby back."

CHAPTER FIFTY-FOUR

"You've got thirty minutes," she says. We're parked at the head of the trail that leads into the meadow behind Lachlan's house. "Good luck."

I get out of the car and look out across the moonlit landscape. Thirty minutes till I hold my baby again. Thirty minutes till this is all over.

I watch her drive away. It's only when she's gone that I realize that I don't have a phone or a watch. I have no way of telling when thirty minutes have passed. And no way of contacting Helen.

In thirty minutes, she's going to knock on his door and distract him. But if I'm early or late, then he'll find me in his house, trying to take his baby, and he'll kill me.

This is a shitty plan, I think.

I count the seconds as I follow the trail, humming the theme song to *Suits.* When this is over, I'm going to lie in bed with my daughter for three straight months, binging TV and junk food like a shut-in.

I'm starting the *Friends* theme song when I see the trail curve sharply away from the houses. Ahead of me is a shallow creek. This is the part I was dreading most. I lift up my jacket and wade through the water, unable to stop myself from yelling out in pain from the freezing temperature of the water. When I get to the other side, I feel my vision clouding over.

Not a good time to pass out, I tell myself, kneeling in the dirt.

I think of Lydia, alone with that man. If I don't do this now, then he'll escape and I'll never see her again. I can't stop now.

When my vision clears, I stand back up and push through the vegetation. I soon reach the back fence of Lachlan's house.

Like the front of the house, the back fence is topped with spikes to prevent anyone from climbing over. It will be impossible to scale, but that was never my plan. Because right next to Lachlan's absurd fence is the fence of our neighbor, which — like all the other fences backing onto the meadow — is only a few feet high.

I'm soon standing in the large backyard of the neighbor's house. This yard is mostly just grass, with a trampoline in the corner and a smattering of abandoned toys. In the trees, I can see a small playhouse.

I stride across the lawn to the fence, then curse. The fence is taller than I remember. Though it isn't covered in spikes, the surface is smooth and it's still beyond my capacity to climb, especially given how weak I am.

I search for a miracle — a ladder, maybe. But as I look around, all I see are two eyes, peering at me from the playhouse.

Great, I think. This is just what I need. A screaming kid warning Lachlan that I'm here.

"Hello?" I ask. "Do you remember me? My name is Olivia."

"My Mom's name is Lisa."

"That's great. I'm the woman who lives next door."

He scratches himself for a moment. "Your cat's name is Homer."

"That's right!" I say. "I've lost my key and can't get inside. Do your parents have a ladder I can use?"

"I can ask!" he says, enthusiastically.

"No, no," I say. "Don't ask them. I'm just wondering how to get over the fence."

"You want to get over there?"

"Yes. I have a baby in there. Would you like to meet her one day?"

"That's easy," he says. He comes out of the playhouse and walks to a bush running along the bottom third of the fenceline. He squeezes past it, then turns his head and waves at me. I follow him, wincing at the scratches along my arm. This is a route for preschoolers, not adults. But when I get beyond the hedge, I see my miracle.

Because there, at the bottom of the fence, is a gate connecting the two properties. This must have been how he got into our garden, all those months ago. There's a piece of wood acting as a makeshift lock. He lifts it up and pushes the gate open.

"Thank you!" I say, but the boy is already squeezing past me.

"I have to go. Did you know it's way past my bedtime?"

I'm about to tell him not to mention me to his parents,

but then I think it might not be such a problem if they call 911. "Thank you."

I'm soon through the gate and into the thick bush next to the chapel. I push through — getting another dozen scratches on my arms in the process — and find myself standing about twenty feet from the house.

My heart begins to race. Everything in me wants to sprint away from this place and never see it again. A voice inside me screams at me to leave.

But I have to fight it. He has my daughter. Nothing else matters.

I walk softly towards the back door. Has it been thirty minutes? I stopped counting. There's a light on in the upstairs bedroom, and I think I see a figure. I freeze, though with the lights on inside there's no way anyone could see me.

For a second, I think it's Anya — but then I remember what I did, and it's like I'm being doused in ice cold water.

A melon, smashed.

I killed her. I've killed a human being. On purpose.

I'm a murderer.

Enough, I instruct my mind. *There'll be time to think of her later. A lifetime to remember.*

I shake my head and keep watching the figure in the window. They turn, and I see that it's Lachlan. His lips are moving. His arms are cradled.

He's singing to her, like a normal doting father.

I want to scream at him, to rush up the stairs and rip her from his arms.

But then I hear a noise. The doorbell. It must be Helen. He turns sharply, then places Lydia down.

This is it. My thirty minutes are up.

It's time to get my daughter back.

CHAPTER FIFTY-FIVE

I hold my breath as I step into the light by the upstairs window, as if it will set off an alarm. But nothing happens, and so I move as quickly as I can to the back door.

I can see the kitchen through the window. All I need to do is creep in quietly and get through to the stairs. Helen is going to attempt to lead him away from the house, but even if that doesn't work, I'm sure I'll be able to get upstairs without being noticed.

Getting down again will be another story. If Lydia cries and Lachlan is still at the door, I won't be able to go down the stairs in time. I'll have to barricade myself in the bathroom. Helen said she'll call the cops — so I'll just have to pray that I survive until they get here.

I'll protect Lydia. Even if I have to give my life, I'll make sure she isn't raised by that brute.

But when I get to the door, my heart sinks.

Because it's locked.

Somehow, I never thought that he'd bother to lock the door. Why would he, given all the security around here?

I give it a few pushes, then look around frantically. There's only one other way inside, and that's through the front door.

Unless.

I look out into the moonlit yard, remembering my conversation with the little boy next door. A ladder. I could use a ladder to climb up to Lydia's bedroom.

The gardener used one to prune the trees. Where did he put it? Down the side of the house?

Yes!

I sprint around the fruit trees and see it stashed out in the open. It's wedged between a pile of spare tiles for the roof and the side of the house, and it's covered in spider webs. I pull it out as gently as I can, though I'm not strong enough to keep it from scraping along the concrete.

By the time I get it to the house, minutes have passed. Am I too late? I can't hear Lachlan, but Helen might have drawn him away from the house.

It doesn't matter. I can't stop now. If he kills me, then he'll go to jail and Lydia will be taken away to be raised by someone else. I feel strangely calm as I think about Lydia growing up somewhere normal, away from Lachlan, away from Rosford.

I extend the ladder and then attempt to quietly lean it against the house. But when I stand it up, it's too heavy for me to control, and it slams against the exterior wall.

I hold my breath. Is that it? Is it over? But I don't hear anything.

I look up the ladder and feel another wave of exhaustion. There's one more problem. How am I going to open the window? There's no elegant way to go about it. I'm going to have to smash it, then hope like hell that Helen has drawn him out of earshot.

I race back around the side of the house, ignoring again how light-headed I am, and grab one of the spare roof tiles. Before I climb the ladder, I pull off my jacket and wrap it around my hand so that I don't cut myself on the glass.

I climb carefully, trying to ignore how unstable the ladder feels. I hadn't propped it very well and as I get higher, I feel how close it is to slipping.

At the top, I pause. The wind whistles. A dog barks.

No signs of Lachlan.

The window is heavy and double-glazed, which means there's no point trying to make this quiet. It'll take all my strength to get the window open. I lift my arm and slam the tile into the glass. A crack extends like a spider's thread — but it's not enough. So I slam it again, and then again.

In the quiet of the neighborhood, the sound is violently loud. I almost feel like I'm on a stage, and that every sound is projected for miles around. That everyone around is listening, watching, open-mouthed.

When it finally smashes, I use my covered fist to clear away the glass. Even so, as I crawl through the open space, I feel small shards tearing into the flesh on my legs. I'm in agony.

But suddenly, miraculously, it doesn't matter anymore.

Because I've found my baby.

Lydia is lying in a wooden bassinet against the wall. Above, a mobile projects soft light across the room. There's a machine in the corner blasting white noise.

And then, she's in my arms. I feel it physically, my love for this girl. I'll never leave her again, never stop protecting her. Even if it kills me.

I move to the window, astonished at how light she is. How can the most important life in the world — *in the entire history of the world* — be so small, so helpless?

I open the window, then look down at the ladder. It's too unstable. I can't risk it. If I fell from this height, I might not be able to stop her from getting hurt.

But then I hear a roar of anger, followed by my name.

"Olivia!"

CHAPTER FIFTY-SIX

I hesitate.

The ladder is too dangerous. But he's in the house. If I try to go down the internal stairs, I'll run straight into him.

The third option? Barricade myself in the bathroom and hope like hell the police come before he kills me.

I have to risk it. There's a front pack tossed on the single bed in the corner of the room. I grab and quickly attach it with Lydia inside. I have a vague sense that she's too young to be carried like this, but I have no choice.

She stirs a little, so I shush her as I move to the window. I open it wide so I don't have to worry about the glass, and hold Lydia close with my right hand as I extend my leg. It's awkward, but I manage to find my footing. I slide out on my side, holding tight to the window sill with my left hand and eventually manage to place my other foot on the ladder.

It doesn't feel secure, but I've only got seconds till Lachlan forces his way through the door. I take a breath, then move my left hand to the ladder and carefully step down, keeping my right hand tucked around Lydia's head. I comfort myself knowing that if I fall, I'll likely land on my back, which will give her a chance of surviving.

As I take another step, the ladder buckles, but I don't stop. I keep moving down. When I'm three feet from the ground, the ladder suddenly slips from under me. I manage to jump away as it falls to the side, slamming against the neighbor's fence.

"My baby," I whisper, and immediately touch Lydia's head. "Are you OK?"

She moans softly, just before her father screams at me from the upstairs window.

"Olivia!"

His voice rings out across the neighborhood. The sound of glass, the crash of the ladder, a screaming husband — it wouldn't take much more to have the police around in a place like Rosford.

I scramble up, just as he disappears from view. Lydia is moaning now, and Lachlan will be downstairs in seconds. I quickly push through the hedge to the gate to the neighbor's yard. In a few seconds I'll be free.

But as I reach the gate, my heart sinks.

It's locked. The piece of wood on the other side of the fence must have slipped down. If I was stronger, I might be able to push through — but with Lydia, I have no chance.

I push back through the hedge, panicking.

Where can I go? Not the back fence, which is also locked. Not the fence to the other neighbor, which is too high to climb.

He'll be here in seconds. I have no choice.

I duck into the only place left. The Sanctuary.

As I burst inside, I see that my easel is still there, along with all my implements. The brushes, the painting knife, the line of paints. It's almost sweet how he still has this fantasy for me. The doting wife and mother, who paints flowers and still life in her free time.

I go behind the altar and pull at the cupboard where I stored my paintings all those months ago, and crawl inside. It feels like another life — a selfish life, now that I have Lydia beside me. I still yearn to paint, but it will be different next time. I won't rely on a man to give me the life I want, even if I have to work twice as hard. I'll do it all myself. Just me and Lydia.

"Mew!"

As if he were reading my mind, Homer trots into view just as I'm closing the cupboard door. I hiss like a snake to try to scare him away — but Homer's a cat, and the last thing he wants to do is take instruction. He mews insistently at the door.

"Yes, I miss you too," I whisper. "Now go away."

Homer stares at me, seemingly insulted by my behavior, then leaps onto the altar and proceeds to lick his paws.

I almost smile — but then my blood runs cold.

"Come out, darling."

I didn't hear him come in. With the echo in the chapel, his voice already sounds close. I keep watching through the slit in the door. When he comes into view, he's standing by my easel. There's a scratch on his face, and his nose is bleeding.

"Come out, my love. I just want to talk."

He must have seen me come in. What can I do now? If I stay here, he'll take Lydia, then kill me. I have to distract him. And that means leaving my daughter on her own.

I quietly undo the straps to my front pack and lay Lydia down on the cupboard floor. She makes a noise and I hear Lachlan's footsteps on the floorboards of the chapel.

"It's OK, baby," I whisper. "Mommy is here. I'll be right back. This will all be over."

I crawl out of the cupboard and close the door behind me.

"Fine," I say. I try to keep my voice from shaking. I'm not scared of this man anymore. All that matters is my daughter. I don't care what he does to me, as long as I keep her safe. "Here I am."

He's standing in the middle of the pews. His face is gray, the color of ash, streaked with lines of crimson.

"What happened to Anya?" he says.

"What happened to Helen?" I counter, my voice shaking. "Did she do that to you?"

"She's not a problem anymore."

"What does that mean?" I ask, though I know the answer. My voice cracks. I suddenly feel cold. I asked Helen to help me — and now she's dead. This is my fault.

Another body.

Another domino falls.

"Where's Anya?"

I tighten my fists. Though I can barely stand, I want nothing more than to hurt this man for everything he has done. Not just to me, but to Helen.

And my daughter — I can't let him hurt my daughter.

"I killed her."

He curls his upper lip. "Impossible. It's not in your nature."

"She was going to throw me off the roof of the art

gallery." I pause, trying to fill my voice with bravado. "So I killed her."

He stares at me for a second, frowning slightly, as if I were an optical illusion that he's seeing clearly for the first time.

"You know," he says, striding towards me. "I used to think you were special. I thought you were wife material. I tried so hard to make you see your potential. The wife and mother you could be. The life we could have had. But I was wrong, wasn't I?"

As he moves, I back away, keeping the pews between us, trying to maneuver him away from the altar. Away from Lydia. I end up back near the entrance. I could break for the door — without Lydia, I might be able to sprint through the house to the front door. I might be able to get away.

But I'm not going to leave her. Never again.

"You're not a wife, though. You're just a slut waitress." He lunges for me, and I duck out of the way. "All those months in the basement, I didn't even touch you. Because I respected you! What a joke."

He lunges for me again, and this time grabs hold of my wrist. I try to pull away, but I'm too weak. He pulls me close and wraps both arms around me, pinning my hands to my waist. As I struggle to get free, he whispers in my ear. "I'm not going to make that mistake twice."

His hands drop and I try to step away — but he pulls me back easily. Then, he grabs my shirt and rips it open, before tossing me to the ground.

And then he's on me. He's pulling at my clothes — and I'm suddenly exposed, helpless underneath him. I scratch at his face, but he overpowers me with ease. I'm still too weak.

He manages to collect my wrists in one hand and with the other, he fumbles with his belt.

I scream, and then I hear Lydia screaming — us, together, against this monster. But neither of us is strong enough to change what's going to happen. What must happen.

I'm too weak to fight him. This is the final domino, the last necessary act.

I look up, and see the name still painted on the rafters.

Yasmin.

I can feel her inside me, pleading.

Get vengeance.

Make the fucker pay.

I can't let it end this way. With all the energy I have left, I free one of my arms and with two fingers poke him directly in his eyes. He cries out and loosens his grip, allowing me to wriggle backwards from beneath him. He grabs me almost immediately, and I slam back against the easel, causing it to topple over. My paint supplies scatter across the floor.

"No more," he grunts, squashing me down. I don't know if this is desire, or just another punishment for his imperfect wife.

Either way, I can't stop fighting.

I manage to keep one arm free, but it doesn't matter. He's on me and his weight is too much. I can't move. I feel him against me. So close.

Just as he's about to push into me, I reach around with my free hand in a panic. There are paint brushes scattered all around, but that's not what I need. I keep sweeping the floor with my hand until I find something sharp.

My painting knife.

I relax my body so he doesn't suspect anything, and just as he tries to move, I slam the knife into the side of his neck.

He cries out, but he's in no position to push me away, so I do it again, and then again, and again.

I keep going until my hand is so covered in his blood that the knife slips from my grasp.

He spasms on top of me, a heavy senseless weight, no longer making a sound.

And then he's still, and it's over.

CHAPTER FIFTY-SEVEN

SIX MONTHS LATER

I love my new life.

I'm in Brooklyn now, in an insanely expensive three-bedroom townhouse that I purchased with some of Lachlan's estate.

I'm a rich woman, but that doesn't matter. All I ever need is a room of my own, and my baby.

And, yes, Homer too. I think he's the only one that misses our life in Rosford, though he's becoming used to life in the city again. Unlike our old Queens apartment, I have a small backyard here. At night, he goes out and explores the neighborhood. Every now and then, I stroke his poor, deformed tail and feel a surge of anger. But Lachlan's gone for good, and can never hurt anyone I love ever again.

Not me. Not Lydia.

I walk up to my studio — a converted room at the top floor of the house — and begin to sketch. Lydia is asleep, which on a good day gives me about two hours to work. She's a strangely calm and peaceful child, despite the drama that brought her into the world.

Every time I work, I think about the other people Lachlan killed. Anya too, of course. Even though I pushed her off the edge, I've been convinced by a therapist that Lachlan was her actual killer.

There's Damian, my ex. He was an asshole, but he didn't deserve to be killed like that.

And Helen? He hadn't killed her, thankfully. When Lachlan heard me smash the window to get into Lydia's room, she attacked him, all to buy me a few more seconds. He knocked her out with a punch to the temple, but it didn't do any lasting damage.

After I moved to Brooklyn, she came to visit me, perhaps on the assumption that we might be friends. It was an awkward afternoon. I'm rusty when it comes to small talk, and our conversation ended up orbiting the only thing we had in common, that black hole that neither of us wanted to draw attention to.

Homer comes into the room and silently curls around my leg.

What other victims were there?

Dr. Yang went to prison after I told the police what he'd done. So did Jack, who knew what Lachlan was doing and helped cover it up. I think of them as his victims, too. Dr. Yang was blackmailed — and so, as it turned out, was Jack. Lachlan had videos of Jack sleeping with much younger women, and had used them to buy his cooperation and silence.

I don't feel sorry for either of them, but I don't hate them for what they did. Not anymore.

My hate goes to only one person, and he's dead.

After Lachlan died, I went through the bizarre process of inheriting his estate. His sister flew to New York, and we sat in the spotless grey offices of a law firm while we went through his assets — his only living relative and his killer. Part of me wanted to surrender my claim to any of it, but I knew that his money would be useful to Lydia, so I went through with the process.

Afterwards, we were stuck together in an elevator, and his sister started telling me about his childhood. How after their father died, he transferred all his affections onto his mother. When she died, his childhood was effectively over. They lived with relatives until they finished high school, but he never got over it. She told me all this quickly, as if his childhood trauma and the death of Yasmin were enough to explain what he'd done to me.

But now, as I think about her story, I don't think it is enough. Between this explanation and everything he did to me is a yawning gap. Something that doesn't easily fit the logic of cause and effect. Some dark potential in the human soul, some latent evil.

Homer whines, so I sit down on the couch and let him jump onto my lap. As he moves in circles, his claws plucking painfully through my skirt, I think of the other victim.

My one-time rival. My mirror. My ghost.

Yasmin.

If I'm honest, she's the only person I truly think about when I paint. She's the person I'm always searching for. Technically, she died in childbirth — but that only happened because she spent her pregnancy locked up, just like me. She's another of his victims. Maybe the first.

Now that the police and lawyers have gone and my life is quiet again, I can't stop thinking about her.

I turn back to the half-finished sketch. Outside, the

branches of a London plane scratch against the window, like fingers trying to claw their way through the glass.

I told my therapist about these pictures, and she says that I'm looking to find some redemptive meaning to those months in the basement. She says I need to accept that Lachlan was a sociopath, and that I've been through serious trauma, but that I have a long life ahead of me.

You need to focus on your daughter now, she says. *Live for her.*

My mother is more insistent. She says I need to move on.

I go to the window and tap my fingers where the tree's branch is scraping against the glass. What does it mean to 'move on'? I was locked in a basement for my entire pregnancy. I'll never really move on. But I know what she means. If I'm going to be a decent mother, I need to try.

"I'll miss you," I say, looking at the picture.

Lydia calls out. I go to her room and give her a bottle while I sit in the armchair. She's nearly six months old, but ever since Lachlan died, she has refused to breastfeed. He took that away from me.

After she finishes her bottle, I place Lydia on a blanket on the ground. Mom and the therapist are right. I can't be a good mother if I keep obsessing about a dead woman I never even met.

"Goodbye, Yasmin," I whisper, before taking the sketch in my hands and tearing it in half. Later, I'll get rid of the others.

My mind goes quiet. It's like when ambient noise — a lawnmower, a dishwasher, the rain on the roof — disappears. I can hear my own breathing, the gentle movements of Lydia, the silence of my apartment.

I kiss my daughter and wait for Homer to come howling for his dinner.

THANK YOU FOR READING

Did you enjoy reading *The Last Wife*? Please consider leaving a review on Amazon. Your review will help other readers to discover the novel.

ABOUT THE AUTHOR

Matt McGregor is a writer of psychological thrillers from New Zealand. Before becoming a writer, Matt taught English (briefly), ran a nonprofit, worked with maps, and led a marketing team for a tech startup. Now, he mostly spends his time inventing surprising ways to murder his characters, which is totally fine and nothing for you to worry about. When he's not writing in the third person, he likes to explore the local wilderness, swim in the sea, and play with his exhaustingly energetic young children.

Visit Matt on his website: https://mattmcgregor.co/

Made in United States
Cleveland, OH
25 August 2025

19771032R00177